Inklings Book 2018

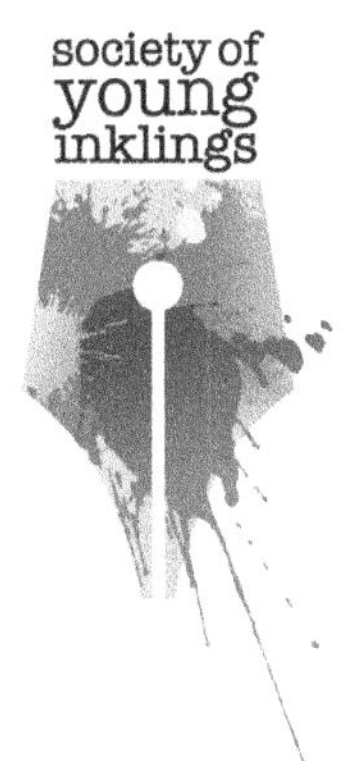

The following young authors contributed their short stories and poems to this anthology.

Ksenia Baatz	Allison Gable	Eva Salvatierra
Anna Birman	Nuala Kilroy	Shinjini Samanta
Jeein Choi	Padma Madhyasta	Ember Summer
Adam Collins	Amann Majahan	Max Wang
Alexa Friesel	Claire McNerney	Anna Yang
Mito Funatsu	Sanjay Ravishankar	Liana Zhu

Thank you to the following mentors for contributing editorial guidance and letters.

Bronté Bettencourt	Alex Doherty	Jena McNealy
Philomena Block	Malar Ganapathiappan	Helen Pyne
Joanna Ho Bradshaw	Jamieson Haverkampf	Sarah Lyn Rogers
Dave Butler	Ailynn Knox-Collins	Sonja Solter
Jenn Castro	Tasslyn Magnusson	Kristi Wright
Ernesto Cisneros	Polly Alice McCann	

Cover illustration by Polly Alice McCann (*www.pollymadison.com*)
Copyedited by Sarah Lyn Rogers
Edited by Naomi Kinsman

Printed in the USA
First Printing: August 2018
ISBN: 978-0-9981849-4-4

Contents

Thank you to our guest judges!

Mandy Davis   Marilyn Hilton   David Shannon   Lauren Wolk

And thank you to our Collaborating Artists!

Rebecca Behrens	Christine Dowd	Shannon Price
Joanna Ho Bradshaw	Marilyn Hilton	Helen Pyne
Dave Butler	Ann Jacobus	Raina Telgemeier
Ernesto Cisneros	Susan Kaye Quinn	Elizabeth Verdick
Kim Culbertson	Patricia Newman	Ashley Walker
Jill Davis	Daria Peoples-Riley	Kristi Wright
Mandy Davis	Mitali Perkins	Anne Young

Foreword

Welcome to the tenth-anniversary edition of the *Inklings Book*! Since 2008, Society of Young Inklings has hosted the annual Inklings Book Contest, a free opportunity for young writers to work with grown-up author-mentors to polish their stories and poems. At the end of this revision process, young writers walk away with the confidence of having their work enthusiastically discussed with a writerly adult, the wisdom of how to apply thoughtful critiques to their current and future writing, and publication in a book featuring their work and work by their peers.

In addition to creative writing, the *Inklings Book* anthology includes a thoughtful "Dear Reader" letter from each author-mentor, explaining the revision strategy chosen for his or her mentee. Whether you are an educator, a young writer, or an author yourself, we hope you will find inspiration in these letters—and in the insightful, imaginative work that follows them.

Selection for the eighteen pieces in this year's anthology was aided by guest judges Mandy Davis, Marilyn Hilton, David Shannon, and Lauren Wolk. The stories and poems that follow were dreamed into being by writers in grades three through nine, and feature pen pals, gnomes, beloved teachers, a dangerous mermaid, magic berries, a tormented artificial intelligence, and cookies that cure heartache.

If you are interested in becoming an Inkling yourself, or one of our Collaborating Artists, you can sign up for a free Society of Young Inklings membership at *www.younginklings.org*. While you're there, feel free to browse our mentorship opportunities, classes, writing prompts, author interviews, and other offerings. We appreciate you being part of our community!

Humor

Bronté Bettencourt worked with Claire McNerney on using humor to break tension and define characters in Claire's story, "Mermaid in the Hot Tub."

Dear Reader,

Humor is a tool more versatile than cracking a simple punchline. In writing, it helps break up the tension in high-stress situations. It can serve as a coping mechanism when a character has a hard time processing difficult information. And the type of humor a character uses tells a lot about their budding personality as they exercise their newfound agency as a young adult. These are all characteristics that define Claire's narrator, Riley (Ri).

When Claire and I sat down to revise "Mermaid in the Hot Tub," we brainstormed about who Ri was. While Ri was having doubts about her her best friend, her best friend was turning into a "were-mermaid." We speculated over what emotions Ri felt, and how those emotions came out through her sense of humor. During the editing process, Claire focused on the ending and what Ri felt after she lost her best friend.

Claire also added details to the world to round out the plausibility of a mermaid appearing in a hot tub in the first place. She added sensory details to ground the characters in her world, as well as to immerse the reader in said world. Details like "purple remnants on her cuticles" and "the grass was thick, but it was slick" create believability in a comical and fantastical scenario.

When Claire writes, she doesn't set out with the intention of being funny. Her humor occurs naturally, with her not forcing her characters to do anything they wouldn't do. My advice would be to get to know your character. If you're writing a funny character, ask why they might be cracking jokes in each situation. Are they feeling nervous? Are they insecure? Are they not taking the situation seriously? From there, you can gain insight into who they are, and once you learn about why they make those decisions, you can write their character more authentically.

Also, take into consideration the way in which the other characters respond to the person cracking the joke. Ri and Beck work well together because their responses to each other's differing senses of humor create the punchline, while also defining who they are as people. By doing this, you're using another method to relay your characters' personalities instead of telling the reader who they are outright.

Happy writing, and may your punchlines ever hit your mark!

Bronté Bettencourt

Bronté Bettencourt graduated from the University of Central Florida with a Bachelor's in English Creative Writing. She is currently pursuing an MFA in Writing for Children and Young Adults at Hamline University. When she is not writing or working, she is a full time D&D enthusiast and YouTube connoisseur. Follow her on Instagram @elliebronte.

Claire McNerney

Claire is fifteen years old and attends Foothill High School. When not writing, she can be found acting, reading, or listening to audio dramas. She likes crafting, producing videos, and contemplating reality (although usually not at the same time). She hopes you enjoy her story and that you have a lovely day. If you want to find her on the internet, her Instagram is @o.h.c.l.a.i.r.e.

Bronté Bettencourt: Why do you enjoy writing?
Claire McNerney: I really, *really* like telling stories and making worlds. I like reading stories, but sometimes the stories that I want to read don't exist, so I make them myself. I like generating ideas. I especially like that moment when you get an idea that you didn't know you needed, that ends up fixing the story.

Q: What was the inspiration for "Mermaid in the Hot Tub"?
A: Our house has a hot tub. So, when I was watching the rain I could totally picture a mermaid in the hot tub. At first, I wanted to put a mermaid in the bathtub, but then I thought, "How would it get there?" (I still confuse the two from time to time.) It made more sense for the mermaid to appear in the hot tub.

Q: How did you go about your revisions with "Mermaid in the Hot Tub"?

A: The big thing that we did was with the ending, adding a couple more paragraphs. We also added a bit more with Beck's character. The new ending added more closure, and it was a good experience to work with a mentor who could see what needed to be added to the story.

Q: What do you think Ri's sense of humor adds to the story?

A: Ri's sense of humor is her personality. It's who she is. Besides being the majority of who she is as a person, her humor makes it so that it's not super ridiculously intense with her friend kind of dying. Her humor is a coping mechanism for her, which comes across in the story. It makes her relatable and understandable.

Q: What advice do you have for other Inklings who don't like revision very much?

A: I get that revising is hard because it's your story, and that you think it's the best thing in the universe. But nothing is the best thing in the universe. There are things that could make your story better, to add more to it. Don't settle for average; you can at least get your story to an A-!

Mermaid in the Hot Tub

by
Claire McNerney

Last Thursday, it rained so hard I thought the backyard would turn into a lake. It didn't, unfortunately, but it did flood the hot tub. You see, I was swimming in it before the rain started, but when it started to thunder, I went back into the house without covering it. It's been a couple of days, and no one's checked on it, because the hot tub is around the corner of the house, in the side yard. You can't see it from inside, and it's been so wet that nobody's visited it since me.

I thought I would get in and go for a swim, so I put my bathing suit on and went out. I walked up the steps and peered into the mucky, pond-scum-covered water. I would have gotten in, but there was just one tiny, itty bitty little problem: There was a mermaid in my hot tub.

She wasn't even that pretty. Beck always said that mermaids were pretty, and that's why she would be one. But this mermaid's skin was scaly, and she looked sickly. There was a disgusting green scum over the hot tub that I thought might be her barf. Or worse. I didn't know, I wasn't the mermaid expert. That was Beck. So I called her, to

tell her about the mermaid. Our conversation went something like this:

Beck: Ugh, Ri! I'm in the middle of my painting my toes, so make it quick. I've got to get the third layer on fast. Ma'll be back in twenty minutes and I need to have socks on before that. You know how crazy she went last time she saw me with nail polish on.

Me: Never mind your nails, Beck. I've got some real news.

Beck: Yeah, sure you do. So? What is it? Did that cute guy from bio call? I knew it! He totally likes you.

Me: No, Beck, don't be ridiculous. There's a mermaid in my hot tub.

I don't know why I whispered the last part, but for some reason, I didn't want anyone else to know. I wanted the mermaid to be my secret. The only reason I told Beck was because she's been obsessed with mermaids since second grade, and I needed some expert advice on what to do with her.

Beck didn't believe me, of course.

Me: No, really. A mermaid. She's kinda ugly, though.

Beck: Then she's not a real mermaid.

Me: Well, why don't you come over here and tell me that after you've seen her.

Beck: Ugh, fine. Be there in ten.

Beck lives down the street, which is probably why we're friends. I don't want to sound cynical, but if you've been friends since preschool, either your parents are friends or you live on the same street. Honestly, if it weren't for our geographical proximity to each other, Beck and I probably wouldn't be friends. We have next to nothing in common. Well, we're both girls, I guess. But she's a girly girl. She loves her nail polish, despite her mom's claims that glamor of any kind is the influence of Satan. I'm not as crazy as her mom, but I despise putting on nail polish. Beck puts it on me sometimes, but I take it off almost immediately. I can't help but to pick at my fingers. It's so annoying.

Beck was over in ten, just like she said. She may have flaws, but she is punctual. Her freshly painted toenails were hidden behind muddy rain boots, her ponytail falling out in the mist.

"Well?" she said. "Show me your stupid mermaid."

I led her back. The mermaid had sunk under the pond scum, but I could see the silhouette of her form beneath the water.

"No mermaid, just like I thought. Really, Ri. How would a mermaid even get out here? We're a hundred miles from the sea."

"You know how sometimes it rains frogs?" I said. It was a long shot.

"No." Of course she didn't.

"Well, it happens. The frogs are sucked up into a storm and when it rains, they fall from the sky, sometimes hundreds of miles from where they started."

"You think that happened, but with a mermaid?" Beck didn't believe me. I nodded, but all she did was roll her eyes.

"Really, Beck. I swear there's a mermaid under there. Look!" I pointed at the shadow under the pond scum. Slowly but surely, it started to move. Beck stood to the side, glaring off into the distance.

"I can't believe you called me here for nothing. Ma won't be

out of the house for another week. When am I ever supposed to paint my nails?" The mermaid started to swim towards her.

"Beck! Turn around, please! She's going towards you!"

"Come on, Ri! It's just a gross hot tub. There aren't any mermaids in here! Grow up." She took one step to walk away, but it was too late. The mermaid surfaced. I could see her teeth, sharp and glowing, even in the muted light of the overcast afternoon.

"Watch out!" It was too late. The mermaid bit down, her teeth scraping Beck's arm. Beck jumped back in pain, screaming. The mermaid hissed before sinking down into the water, only her eyes and the fin on her head visible above the pond scum.

"There's a mermaid in your hot tub," Beck said, as if I hadn't been trying to tell her that for the past twenty minutes.

"I know," I said.

"The mermaid in your hot tub bit me," she said again, like I didn't have eyes.

"Yeah. I know. Are you all right?" I took hold of her arm where the mermaid had bitten her. It was bleeding a little bit and green and brown around the edges.

"Not really," she said. "It kinda hurts." I touched it. "Ow!"

"Well, come on. Let's go clean it." I led her around the side yard towards the house.

"There's a mermaid in your hot tub and she bit me and it hurts," Beck repeated.

"I know," I said. She really must have been in shock. It was like she didn't even register me as a fellow human being.

"Well, what are you going to do about it?" Finally, a good question. I could only wish I knew the answer.

I tried my hardest to clean Beck's cut out, but she whined that "it hurt" every time I touched it. So I just slapped an old Hello Kitty bandaid on it and hoped for the best. She put purple polish on her pinky fingernail before going home for dinner, claiming that she wouldn't be able to do it anywhere else. After she left, I stayed in my room, avoiding my mother and worrying about the mermaid problem.

I came up with two ideas to tell Beck in the bus to school the next day. I didn't really think she'd like any of them, but they slowed my worrying down enough so that I could actually sleep.

The first involved a wheelbarrow and St. Elmo's Creek. I figured we could probably bait the mermaid into the wheelbarrow and wheel it two miles down the hill to St. Elmo's Creek. It was an iffy plan, but better than my alternative.

See, I figured the mermaid must have attacked Beck for a reason. It could have been her hair, or the color of her shirt or whatever, but I'm pretty sure that it was the toxic smell of her wet nail polish under her rain boots. It was very possible that she attacked it because she was afraid of it. And if she was afraid of it, that meant it could probably hurt her. The plan was vague, but I figured we could buy a bottle of cheap nail polish and empty it into the hot tub or something.

When I told Beck about that one, her eyes bulged. "You'd really kill it?"

"I don't want to, but it could be dangerous. If we can't get it to St. Elmo's, it could be the only option. It's already attacked you. Who knows what it might do next?"

Beck pulled her sleeves further down her arms. "Listen, Ri. This mermaid you got is no joke. You should tell someone."

"Who? My mom? She'd send me to a mental facility!"

"I dunno, maybe the police could help," Beck said, but she was barely hanging onto her argument. "Okay, okay, fine. I get it. No one's going to help. But how in the heck are you going to get that mermaid all the way to St. Elmo's Creek?"

"I told you, I dunno yet. But we've got a wheelbarrow, and it can't be too hard, right?" Beck rolled her eyes.

"You're too optimistic, Ri. Also, you're insane."

"Oh well, too bad." I said as I zipped up my backpack. "You're stuck with me."

When I saw Beck again, it was bio, right before lunch. She smiled and waved and teased me about the guy in the back that she thought liked me, but something was off. She asked to borrow a pencil, which was nothing new, but when she reached out to grab it, I spotted something green on the back of her hand.

"What's that?"

"Oh, nothing." She tried to pull her hand away but I caught it. Shiny green scales—flecked with the rust of dried blood at the edges—appeared from under Beck's sleeve. I reached out to touch them, but she pulled her hand away again, successfully this time.

"Beck," I said cautiously. "Are there *scales* on your arm?"

"Not so loud!" she whispered, just as loud as I was. "Do you want everyone from here to Timbuktu to know?"

"How?"

"I don't know, they just appeared overnight. They spread out from my bite mark . . . look, there's some on my neck, too." She brushed her hair away, revealing several sparkling scales that wove their way up her neck behind her ear.

"Won't they come off?" I asked.

"Don't you think I've tried?" She set her hand down on the table. Her fingernails were broken and covered in dry blood. Her pinky fingers, once glossy, were the worst of all. The only evidence that they were ever even polished was the purple remnants in her cuticles. Beck had bitten off her own nail polish. *Beck.* I was horrified to see her pick at her cuticles as she continued to speak. "They won't come off. It's like they're part of my skin."

"Do you think . . . "

"No, I know." Beck said, not taking her eyes off mine. "That mermaid did this to me. I don't know if there was poison in her teeth or if it got infected with some bizarre scale-y disease, but somehow she did this to me."

I didn't know how to respond. This meant that the mermaid was actually something serious. Something scary. Something that had to be handled with caution. But before I could come up with an eloquent response, Beck spoke.

"We should try your wheelbarrow idea," she said.

"How are we going to get her out of the hot tub?" I asked. "There's a reason we haven't done it yet."

"Ladies, would you like to share your conversation with the class?" The teacher glared from the whiteboard.

"No, ma'am. Sorry, ma'am," Beck and I replied in synch. The moment the teacher turned her back, Beck faced me.

Don't worry; I've got a plan, she mouthed. When I gave her a look, all she did was wink at me, and go back to taking notes.

All through bio, I couldn't concentrate. What was Beck's plan? Why was she so confident and calm when her arm was covered in scales? And about the scales—what was up with that? Would she turn into some kind of were-mermaid? The lesson had never felt further away.

When the lunch bell finally rang, Beck was all ready to go. She tapped her nails impatiently against the top of the desk. "Come on, Ri. Hurry up!"

"Why are you so excited for lunch?" I asked, zipping up my backpack.

"Oh no, Ri. We're not going to lunch," she said as we walked out of the room. "Quickly now. Carl's waiting."

Carl was Beck's older brother, in town for the week from college. He owned a disgusting car and always wore a baseball cap. When I was little, I used to imagine that he had tentacles for hair, or snakes, and that he had to wear the baseball cap to keep them away from the sunlight, because they burned easily. I still have no idea what color his hair is beneath that cap. Some things just aren't meant to be known.

We got into Carl's crusty brown hatchback at the bottom of the hill. My stomach turned as he started the car, sending a shudder throughout the entire vehicle.

"Just to Ri's house," Beck said. Carl grunted. Despite everything, he still scared me.

The car made its way through the fog to my house. I say "the car" instead of "Carl" because it didn't really feel like he was in control of it. It was so bumpy that I could feel every crack in the asphalt, and every time we turned a corner, Beck slid into me. But by some miracle, the car got us to my house.

As we got out, Beck whispered something in Carl's ear. He shrugged and grunted, and slouched further into the front seat.

"Grab your wheelbarrow," Beck said, scale-covered hands on her hips. Had the scales grown further since bio? "Let's get this mermaid out of here."

"You still haven't told me how you're going to get her out of the hot tub," I said, frustrated. "How are we supposed to get her out if I don't know the plan?"

"I've got a plan, don't worry. Come on, Ri. Where do you keep it?" Beck made her way towards the hot tub.

"Why don't you just tell me?" I asked.

"We need to hurry." She scratched the scales on her arm.

"Tell me the plan, or I won't help you at all. I'm fine with having a mermaid in my hot tub." I wasn't, but Beck couldn't know that. There was absolutely no reason for her to not to tell me. It was my hot tub and my wheelbarrow. She was being completely unreasonable.

"Where's the wheelbarrow?"

"Are you even listening to me?" I stood still, hands at my side. Beck turned around and walked towards me.

"Listen, I don't have much time." Beck leaned towards me, spitting slightly in my face. "We need to do this quickly. So, tell me, Riley. Where is the wheelbarrow?"

I shook slightly. "What do you mean you don't have enough time?"

Beck sighed. "Do you have to be annoying about this, Ri?" She pulled off her jacket. Her hands were completely scaly, her fingers starting to curve. She took the hem of her sweater and pulled up. Her

shirt thrown to the side, Beck stood in front of me, wearing only her undershirt. But I couldn't see any flesh. Her entire torso was covered with shiny gray-green scales.

"Oh. Beck." I didn't know what else to say. "Oh, no."

"Listen, I know it looks bad, but we can make sure the "mermaid" doesn't do this to anyone else, okay?" She walked away, and I could see a fin growing on her back, spikey and green.

"I'll get the wheelbarrow," I said, and deep in my stomach, a knot began to grow.

❁

I raced out and around to the back shed, where the wheelbarrow sat. It was orange and slightly rusty. Beck and I used to play in this shed. We used the wheelbarrow as a boat when we went out sailing for mermaids. Funny. Beck was always so obsessed with mermaids, but I don't think she ever really wanted to *become* one. Not in this way, at least.

As I rolled the wheelbarrow out, I heard a hissing noise from the hot tub area, followed by Beck's scream. I wheeled the barrow a little bit faster.

The hot tub sat open, the pond scum just as thick as it had been when I left it, except this time it looked a little . . . purple? Beck stood near the edge, holding a pole and emptying a bottle of purple nail polish into the water. The mermaid was nowhere to be seen.

When Beck saw me, she shouted, "Over here! She tried to attack me again, but I pushed her underwater. I think she'll be popping back up again soon! When she does, I'm going to take this pole and knock her into the wheelbarrow. Got it?"

18

I nodded. To be honest, I was a little bit numb. Everything seemed to be happening so fast and so out of my control.

Mermaid Beck, who seemed to think she was going to die any moment now, lifted the pole. She still hadn't put her sweater back on (it must have been uncomfortable with her fin), and her scales glinted in the light. It was kind of fascinating, the scales. Of course, I wished they weren't there, I'm not that horrible of a person, but I couldn't help staring. It was so hard to believe that there were scales on Beck . . . scales that had replaced her skin and couldn't be pulled off. Scales that might be there forever.

"Get into position!" Beck shouted. "I see bubbles!"

I bent my knees, completely unprepared. I could feel my heartbeat in my ears, thumping loudly. I briefly wondered if Beck still had a heartbeat. Or ears. I looked over at her. Her hair, dark and silky and meticulously combed, covered where her ears would be, but I could see that the scales had grown up her neck and onto her chin and the sides of her face.

And then I saw her swing the pole like a baseball bat. And the mermaid's claws reached out for her face but it was too late. My eyes followed the creature as she flew across the hot tub and, by some miracle, landed in the wheelbarrow.

I may have screamed.

The mermaid tossed and turned like the fish that she was, trying to get out of the wheelbarrow, but she was too slippery, and so the wheelbarrow held. Beck shoved me out of the way, grabbed the wheelbarrow, and started to run through the side yard.

"Come on!"

Carl was still slouched in the car, but when he saw Beck

coming, he popped the trunk and started the engine. I helped Beck put the entire wheelbarrow into the hatchback. The mermaid almost escaped, but Beck smashed her fist into its nose, or where its nose would be if it were human. I vividly remember the glint in her eye as she turned to me with a smile. "Just like a shark!" she said, too excited.

Before I had even buckled my seatbelt, Carl started to drive. The mermaid's hissing and screeching was even louder than the engine. The car lurched at every turn. Beck was turned backwards, holding on to the backseat headrest. Every thirty seconds, she hit the thrashing mermaid with her pole.

And then we were driving down the hill to St. Elmo's creek. Carl parked in the handicap spot at Beck's order. I raced out to open the trunk. Together, we pulled the wheelbarrow out of the car. The mermaid lashed out at Beck again, and she fell backwards.

"God, Beck," I said, "Are you all right?" She popped up and stepped forward, grabbing the wheelbarrow.

"Yeah, fine." Her voice was hoarse and scratchy, like she was having a hard time breathing. "Let's go."

We pushed it over to the side of the stream. The grass was thick, but it was slick, and it wasn't too hard to push the wheelbarrow, especially since the mermaid was now still and silent. When we got to the edge of the creek, I stopped. Beck looked back at me. Scales covered her entire face, her hair was pale, green, and congealing into a fin. I noticed that she didn't have ears anymore.

"Come on, Ri," she said softly. "Let's do it."

And even though her fingers were so clawed she could barely hold her pole, she helped me push the unconscious mermaid out of the wheelbarrow and into the river. Her body floated there, for just a moment, before swimming away.

We collapsed into a heap on the shore, sitting on the damp grass with our feet on the sand.

"Thank you." I hugged her. "You're my best friend."

"You too." She sighed. "Really, Ri. I'm so glad we're friends."

In the center of the creek, there was a splash. For a moment, I saw a fin rising from the water. Beck looked at it, fear in her eyes. But Beck wasn't afraid, was she? She couldn't be. Beck was the fearless one. The one who painted her nails even though her mom wouldn't let her, and dragged me around to all of the clubs at school. Beck couldn't be afraid. But she also couldn't be a mermaid, and she was.

"I have to go," she said, crawling towards the creek. Her legs were fused together, and I noticed purple spots where her toes used to be. "I'm so glad we're friends, Ri." She smiled sadly, her teeth points.

"Beck." She waded in for a few feet before slipping underwater. She turned and smiled at me, as wild as the mermaid we had just let go. I watched my best friend disappear beneath the water. The current flowed far and fast, but I swear I could see a purple-flecked tail fin just beneath the surface. It waved for a moment, and then it was gone.

I got a ride home from Carl. I'm not sure if he was ignoring the fact that Beck wasn't there or if he just genuinely didn't notice. Either way, neither of us said anything during the entire ride, until he pulled up in front of my house. I managed to cough out a thanks before he

continued down the street to his house. Beck's house.

Oh god, Beck. It hadn't really hit me that she wasn't coming back. Wherever she was, whatever she was, it was not something reversible. Beck was gone. As in "I'm-never-going-to-see-her-again-because-she-became-a-mermaid" gone. She would never show up to my house with a bottle of nail polish again, never tease me about boys, never chat with me on the bus, never reminisce about playing mermaids in the wheelbarrow ever again.

Mom made me clean out the hot tub. Beneath all the pond scum and muck, the nail polish Beck poured in during our mermaid relocation was stuck to the sides of the tub. Despite the fact that we drained out all of the water and scrubbed at the nail polish for hours, there was still a purple sheen.

Even after the hot tub had been filled and emptied hundreds of times, the purple polish stain remained. And when I sat in the hot tub and closed my eyes, I could smell the nail polish fumes and see my best friend, Beck, smiling.

Building toward an Emotional Climax

Malar Ganapathiappan mentored Eva Salvatierra through a revision focused on the emotional impact of different stanzas and line breaks in her poem, "My Heart in Black Ink."

Dear Reader,

Poetry often takes you on an emotional journey. Eva's poem is certainly one of those! During our revision, we focused on building the emotions of her poem to a strong climax.

In order to do this, Eva played around with pauses in her poem. Adding breaks in stanzas and lines allowed the imagery to intensify by emphasizing certain phrases and increasing the overall clarity of the piece. Eva was able to use the breaks in stanzas in her revised draft to pack power in the imagery without having the words tumble through to the climax. Managing the speed of the piece controlled the speed for the reader.

Eva tried different break and stanza combinations, noticing how they felt to her until she found the perfect format and the precise language to crisply make a point. Crafting each line and stanza of her poem to build on the emotions helped create a flow from the very first image to the end.

As a writer, it is often difficult to determine which words are unnecessary and to decide which words to take out from a draft. Eva worked on using her strength to create specific images to highlight the most powerful imagery, eliminating any excess words in order to leave the reader with the essence of the piece. Eva did a great job with the changes she made.

If you are working on a poem like Eva, consider the impact of stanzas and line breaks on building an emotional climax. Notice how pause in poetry can allow an image to linger in the reader's mind, amplifying the feeling's weight. And allow yourself to try new things!

Malar Ganapathiappan

Malar Ganapathiappan is a writer, writing mentor with Inklings, writing coach, and member of the Society of Children's Book Writers and Illustrators. She holds a bachelor's degree in psychology. Sharing inspiration, creativity, and perspective through stories gives her joy. When not reading or writing, she enjoys nature, fitness, art, and cats.

Eva Salvatierra

Eva is in eighth grade at Castilleja. In her free time, she loves going on adventures with her friends, writing short stories and poetry, running track, and binging on Netflix. She has a big passion for musical theater, and this year played Elle Woods in the musical *Legally Blonde*. Eva strives to live life to the fullest and can't wait to see where poetry will take her in the future.

Malar Ganapathiappan: How did you get the idea for your poem?

Eva Salvatierra: This poem was inspired from my connection to my two best friends. When one of my friends goes through hard stuff, it feels like I only have words to help her. I don't see her every day, so it's mostly just words on a screen. This poem is a tribute to how I want to strive to make her feel heard and allow people to have the warmth of someone even if they're not there.

Q: How was the revision process for you?

A: I learned a lot about my writing style through it. I learned what my kryptonite was—I like using a lot of unnecessary words. Editing to take out words was difficult for me because it felt like my baby. It's always hard for me to do that, but when you start rearranging it, you see the poem better. Building the emphasis and thinking of it as a story—how you want to build some things, cut down on others, get the rhythm right—I thought about all this.

Q: Where do you get inspiration from?

A: I get inspiration from life experiences. It's after I've been out or done something that I'm in the mood to write.

Q: When did you start writing?

A: Since I was three. I was always telling myself stories and in elementary school, writer's workshop was my favorite thing, drawing inspiration from others' writing. I started writing short stories more recently. I don't like writing nonfiction. I like short stories. And I like writing poetry because I can write about feelings, instead of what happens and dialogue.

Q: What advice might you give to someone for revising poetry?

A: Try to view your poem from a reader's perspective. Be flexible with it. Don't worry–the heart of the poem will still be there even if you're rearranging stuff. Revision can make the poem feel more powerful.

My Heart in Black Ink

by

Eva Salvatierra

Sometimes
there are nights
when words fail me
and all i have left
is a dry tongue
and a snapped pencil

because in the darkness
there is simply
too much
for a glowing screen
or a silver lead
to understand

some nights
you will not need words
you will need
arms to hold you

because in the darkness
some tears
bear a burden
words cannot explain

but i will continue to try
so when my arms
cannot hold you
and when the heaviness
is too thick

you will have
my words
as an anchor
you will have
my heart
in black ink

Building to a Dramatic Climax

Jena McNealy advised Padma Madhyasta on a revision to build dramatic tension and a satisfying arc in her story, "The Golden Berries."

Dear Reader,

For Padma's story, we chose building to a dramatic climax as our revision focus. The climax is the most tension-filled part of the story—the part where your main character faces the main problem of the story. The reader should feel unsure if the main character will get through it!

In the climax of her story, Padma's main character, Patrick, must take drastic measures to deliver important news to the king. In Padma's first draft, Patrick walked straight into the palace to see the king and delivered the news. We decided to add tension and conflict to this scene so it felt more satisfying when Patrick delivered the news.

Padma put herself in Patrick's shoes and I asked her a few questions. What does Patrick see? What does he hear? How does he feel? What does he say to the guards who won't let him through? What do the guards say back? Padma took her new ideas and added them into the scene. Now, Patrick has to overcome a number of obstacles in order to reach the king. Through this revision, Padma discovered a new twist to add to the scene, which brings even more surprise to the climax.

When you're trying to build to a climax, take a moment to think about all that your character has gone through in order to reach this point. Then put yourself in your character's shoes. Ask yourself or have a friend ask you some questions about what's going on. You'll be surprised at what you discover!

Happy revising!
Jena McNealy

Jena McNealy wishes she had the opportunity participate in an Inklings program as a child. As Managing Director of Society of Young Inklings, she strives to extend the opportunity to as many children as possible. Jena began working with Society of Young Inklings in 2010. She holds a BA in creative arts and a minor in education from San José State University. In her spare time, Jena enjoys spending time with her family, traveling, and cooking.

Padma Madhyasta

Padma is nine years old and lives in Fremont, California. She likes drawing, playing sports, watching TV, writing, and reading. She likes writing short stories featuring her family members. She has another book published called *The Little Unicorn*. Her favorite author is Raina Telgemeier.

Jena McNealy: Why do you enjoy writing?
Padma Madhyasta: I can make my dreams come to life.

Q: Where do you like to write?
A: I like writing in a place where nobody will disturb me.

Q: Do you ever feel blocked? What do you do?
A: Yes. When I feel blocked, I leave my story alone for a couple of days and then ideas will come to me.

Q: How did you revise the climax of your story?
A: I pretended I was my main character, Patrick, so I could see what he was seeing and feel what he was feeling. Then I added those details into the story.

Q: What advice do you have for Inklings if they don't like revision very much?

A: I would tell them that revising makes stories even better. I would show them the "before" and "after" climax scene from my story so they could see the changes. I would also tell them to read a book. There are good ideas in books.

The Golden Berries

by

Padma Madhyasta

There was a poor man named Patrick living in a tiny wooden hut near the forest. His wife—Maria—and their five children lived with him. Their hut was made of willow poles and tule grass. The door was made of leather. During the day, Patrick went into the deep forest to hunt for food and gather other supplies for their living. Maria and the children picked berries, fruits, and nuts in the forest, closer to their home. During the night, they all gathered around the fire cooking fish and meat while telling stories about their day. They slept on their leaf mats to the soothing sound of the stream flowing nearby.

But now it was getting more and more difficult to find food. It hadn't rained enough for many years and the big drought was setting in. The animals were starving and the trees and plants were withering. The stream was also drying up. Maria and Patrick thought of moving to the capital of the kingdom where the kind King Louis ruled. But it was not possible to go on such a long journey with

small children without enough food supplies. So, they tried to eat less and save food for their children.

A man with shimmering golden boots, emerald green eyes, and a beautiful diamond crown came walking in the forest one day. He saw a path and continued on there. He found a rock to sit on and ate six loaves of bread. The rock was the favorite spot of Penny, Patrick and Maria's youngest child. As Patrick saw the man, he decided to ask for some bread to feed his hungry family. He thought of asking his wife before approaching the stranger.

"Maria, Maria," Patrick said, "I have good news."

"What is it, darling?" Maria asked.

"I saw a rich man walking down our path and sitting on Penny's favorite rock. He had many loaves of bread with him. I thought of asking him a loaf to feed the kids," Patrick said.

"Oh no, Patrick! Asking for food doesn't look nice. Are you sure about this?" Maria asked, worried.

"Oh, don't worry, Maria. I will ask for only one loaf for the kids," said Patrick. Maria agreed.

Patrick walked out of the house and saw the rich man who had just stood up to continue his journey. But just then, a ferocious lion leapt out of the bushes and began chasing the man.

Patrick had to help, so he said, "Come into this cave here, it's safe here."

The man heard his call and followed it. He hid in the bushes near the cave and the aggressive lion lost track of him. The man quickly went inside the cave. Just then, a group of men carrying weapons fought with the lion and killed it. They were the king's guards.

"Thank you so much for saving my life," said the man to

Patrick. "I am King Louis. I got lost in the forest while hunting and got separated from my group. I have to go back now, but as a reward, here are a few loaves of bread for you."

Patrick was dumbfounded that he was seeing and talking to the King Louis himself. Patrick mumbled nervously, "Thank you so much, King Louis."

"Maria! Maria!" Patrick said softly in excitement, seeing all the kids fast asleep.

His wife came to him and said, "Oh, Patrick, what is it?"

"Oh, look! Oh, look!" said Patrick, pointing to the seven loaves of bread. She smiled so happily, it was like the sun was right behind her. She put it away for the next day and they went to bed.

In the morning, they had ground acorn flour with a loaf of bread for their breakfast. After breakfast, Penny sat on her favorite rock just like she did every day. Next to the rock, Penny found a small golden pouch. Penny was curious and she immediately opened the pouch. In it, she saw several small golden rocks. She picked one of them and it was not a rock. It was soft and squishy to touch just like a berry. Penny ran to her father and showed him the berries.

She said, "Daddy, I found these weird rock-like things, but they actually feel like berries."

"Penny, don't touch them. They may be poisonous. Put them back where you found them," said her father. With great disappointment, Penny put it back in its place.

Coming back home from his hunting trip one day, Patrick was very tired and so he sat on Penny's favorite rock. There he found the golden pouch Penny had showed him a few days ago. He looked inside the pouch. The golden berries looked irresistible to eat. He

hadn't caught anything on his hunting trip. There was not much food left at home, too. So he took one of the berries and ate it. It was very delicious. It instantly made him feel full and he was not hungry or tired anymore. He went home. He did not tell anyone that he ate the golden berry because he thought eating the berry might harm them in some way. He decided to wait and see what happened to him before sharing the golden berries with his family.

Patrick went hunting the next afternoon. In the forest, all around him he could hear different voices talking in low, high, screeching, and soft tones. It took him a while to realize that he was hearing the animals and birds talk. He could understand them! He was very scared. He thought the golden berry created this problem. But as the day passed, he got used to the voices and he liked listening to the animals talk.

As the sun set, Patrick walked back home. Tired, he sat on Penny's favorite rock. All of a sudden, the voices became quiet. Patrick was terrified. He wondered what the berry would do next. It was the same time of the day as yesterday when he had eaten the berry. He was very, very hungry. He decided to eat another golden berry. He ate the berry and voilà! The voices were back again. Patrick realized that the effect from one magic berry lasted for only one day. He decided to not share the berries with his family as they would be frightened by the voices they would hear all day.

One afternoon, Patrick was resting high up in a tree deep in the forest. He heard two lions talking about how King Louis killed their brother. The older lion said, "We shall get our revenge! Every full moon night, the king has dinner with his family in the meadows near his palace. We will attack and kill him then. Next full moon is in three days. We should hunt a big prey to have a good dinner tomorrow and then head to the meadows the next morning." Patrick was shaking in fear after hearing this. But soon, he realized he had to save the king.

That night when the children were asleep, Patrick told Maria all about the golden berries, their magical power, and what he had heard the lions speak.

He said, "Tomorrow morning before the sun rises, I will start my journey to the palace. I do not need any food now. I have a few berries with me. I should be back in six days. Please take care of the children. Don't go deep into the forest. I will try to get some food on my way back. Take care of yourself."

Maria was very worried about how Patrick could take such a long journey in this severe drought. But she knew saving the king was the right thing to do.

Before dawn, Patrick set out for his journey. He walked for miles on the dry, crinkly grass, and dried twigs and leaves. As he walked, he saw all around him. There was barely any greenery left around the place. Everything was dry and barren. At sunset, Patrick settled down near a riverbed under a tree with few green leaves. The river was almost dried up. Patrick was very hungry. He ate a berry and drank some water from the river. As he tried to go to sleep, he heard the tree crying.

With tears in its eyes, the tree talked to Patrick.

"Excuse me, kind sir. Could you please bring me some water from the river? My roots cannot reach deep enough to touch the dried-up river. I have been waiting too long for it to rain. I may fall down and die if I do not get any water today." The tree was very weak and did not have much energy to talk any further.

Patrick gathered a few dried leaves and made a bowl by weaving them together. Little by little, he brought in water in the bowl from the river and poured it at the bottom of the tree trunk. The tree drank the water and seemed to rest peacefully. Patrick was very tired after the many trips to the river and back, so he soon fell fast asleep. In the morning, when Patrick prepared to resume his journey, the tree spoke.

"Thank you very much for saving my life. Here are three seeds for you. I get these seeds only when I am too dried up and about to fall. You can plant these seeds, and the tree that grows out of them will never run out of fruits. If there is drought, you can water it on only two days: one on Christmas, and one on Easter day." Patrick thanked the tree and resumed his journey.

On his way, Patrick heard an animal crying for help.

"Help! Help! Mommy, where are you?" Patrick looked around and saw a well a few feet away. He walked to the well and looked inside it. The well was deep and dried up. At the bottom, he saw a baby rabbit. It was scared and crying. Patrick gathered some dried vines and made a long rope out of them. He threw the rope down into the well. The baby rabbit hung on to the rope and Patrick pulled it out of the well. The baby rabbit was frightened and shaking.

"Where is your mommy?" Patrick asked the rabbit.

The rabbit perked up and pointed to a red barn at a nearby farm. Patrick took the rabbit to the barn. As Patrick was nearing the farm, he heard a rabbit cry.

"Alice, Alice, where are you? Please come back, baby. Mommy misses you a lot."

Patrick put the baby rabbit down on the ground and it ran to its mommy. The rabbits were very happy and jumped around with joy. The farmer came out of his house and was very happy to see the baby rabbit.

"A hawk carried it away earlier in the day and the mommy rabbit has not eaten anything since then. Thank you so much. Where did you find it?" asked the farmer.

"I found it in the well far away from here. The hawk must have dropped it while flying," said Patrick.

Patrick told the farmer that he was going to the palace. The farmer gave him the best of his donkeys for his journey. He also shared some food and water with Patrick. Patrick rested there that night and continued his journey the next day.

Going through meadows, hills, and fields, Patrick approached a small hill. He climbed up the hill, hoping to end his journey on the other side. As soon as he reached the top, he saw the sun glistening brightly against a tall tower.

"The palace!" he shouted with relief and excitement. He was so happy to see the palace that he burst into tears. He galloped down the hill.

"I have arrived! I have arrived!" he screamed with joy. As he got closer to the palace, he heard people laughing and talking, and having a good time. He saw birds flying around happily, chirping and singing. He saw many beautiful buildings and a lot of greenery everywhere. He thought to himself that the people here must never have to worry about hunger. He wished he could live here with his family.

Patrick was very nervous and his knees were shivering as he came to the palace gates.

"What if they don't let me inside the palace?" he worried.

The king's life is in danger and I have to inform him, he thought, gathering up his courage. Patrick told the palace guards what he had heard the lions say. The guards laughed at him. He requested to meet the king directly.

"Oh you fool, you do not belong here. Look at your ragged clothes. Go back to your forest," ordered one of the guards.

Patrick pleaded that he wanted to see the king.

The guards got angrier and shouted at him, "Go back where you came from or else you will be put in the prison." But Patrick did not move back at all. He kept saying that the king was in danger and he had to save him. The guards were now furious. They tied up his hands and took him to the prison.

In the prison, Patrick again pleaded with the prison guards to let him see the king or else the lions would kill the king. Hearing this, one of the prison guards looked at him carefully and suddenly remembered who Patrick was. That guard was with the king in the forest on the day Patrick had saved the king's life from a lion. The prison guard released Patrick and took him to the king.

The king was surprised and happy to see Patrick in the palace. He told everyone the story of how Patrick had saved his life from the lion.

"I did not have anything other than the loaves of bread to give you on that day. I am very glad you came to the palace. Please be our guest for few days and take this small treasure box as a gift for saving my life," said the king.

Patrick said, "Thank you, Your Majesty. But I did not come here for the gift. I am here to warn you of the danger to your life. The family of the lion that you killed is seeking revenge. They will attack you this full moon night when you have dinner in the meadows. I found this pouch in the forest. It must belong to you. I am sorry, Your Majesty, but I was starving, so I ate the golden berries. That is how I could understand the lions talking." The king believed Patrick, as he knew the magical powers of the berries.

That night was the full moon. The king did not go for dinner to the meadows. Instead, the guards laid a trap there and caught and killed the lions. All the people were very thankful to Patrick for saving the king's life again.

When it was time for Patrick to go home, the king loaded a horse carriage full of wealth and food for Patrick to take with him. But Patrick politely declined.

"Your Majesty, I do not want any wealth. It will be stolen by thieves, so my life will be in danger. Instead, I request you to give my family a house and some work here in the capital so that we can live here and serve you," said Patrick.

The king agreed.

Patrick had another request, too. He gave one of the magical seeds to the king and said, "This is a magical seed. When it grows into a tree, it will never run out of fruits. I request you to sow this in the center of the capital, so that all the people, animals, and birds in the capital can eat the fruits when they want and never go hungry."

All the people in the town were happy to hear that. The king sowed the seed in the center square of the capital. That night, it rained very heavily in the capital.

On his way back to his home, Patrick gave a magical seed to the farmer he had met before. He asked the farmer to plant it in

his farm and feed all the people, animals, and birds in his town. He shared the food sent by the king with the farmer and his family. They were all very grateful to Patrick. The farmer sowed the seed in his farm. That night it rained very heavily there.

Maria and the children were very happy to see Patrick back home. They all listened to the stories from Patrick's journey and ate the scrumptious food the king had sent. Patrick told them that they would be living in the capital and that the king had sent three horse carriages with him to take their belongings to their new home. They all jumped for joy.

The next morning, they started gathering and packing their things to take to their new home. Patrick, Maria, and all the children were very sad to leave their home but they were also very excited for the new beginning.

Patrick planted the last magical seed he had, near his home. It was for the animals and birds of the forest with whom he had lived all these years. That night, it rained very heavily in the forest.

Characterization through Dialogue

Alex Doherty encouraged Sanjay Ravishankar to reveal more of his character's personality through dialogue in his story, "A Journey to America."

Dear Reader,

For a writer, one of the most important aspects of storytelling is putting character senses, actions, and dialogue on the page to evoke a deeper connection between the reader and the story.

One of the revision elements Sanjay focused on for his story, "A Journey To America," was showing his characters through their dialogue, and giving them each their own voice. One method he used was expanding on character relationships by adding conversation to replace summary narration.

His story is told from the perspective of a father, bringing his wife and children to a new country. When they are separated, a difficult choice must be made—they can all return home, or his main character can stay in America to provide income.

In the initial version of the story, the decision was made without dialogue, distinctly from the main character's point of view. In Sanjay's revision, we get to see why and how the main character and his wife make the decision for the benefit of their family, by having a conversation.

Sanjay was also able to expand on character with additional dialogue from the guards, doctors, and among his family throughout his short story. By giving each character dialogue, he was able to keep the main character's perspective intact, but give the reader a sense of how other characters felt at the same time.

When you're writing your story, make sure to let your characters speak for themselves, and pose contradictions or challenges to your main character through their dialogue or actions. What people say and do matters, and can give your reader a sense of character without relying on narration.

Write on,
Alex Doherty

Alex Doherty is a writer based in the Bay Area and has an MFA in screenwriting. He worked as a Story Assistant for film and TV production in Los Angeles before working as an Assistant Producer at LucasArts in San Francisco. He's querying his first novel in 2018, a middle grade adventure! He's inspired by the creativity of others and enjoys theater, movies, reading, and finding time to practice his green thumb when he's not hiking.

Sanjay Ravishankar

Sanjay is in fifth grade. He enjoys playing basketball with his sister and dad. He loves to draw and write comic, adventure, and mystery stories. His favorite subjects in school are art, math, and science. Sanjay loves reptiles because they are usually excluded by many and they also are super cool!

Alex Doherty: How did you get into the mind of the main character to tell the story from his perspective?

Sanjay Ravishankar: I tried to look at my story from different perspectives. My main character had the most adventure possibility, living in a new country and giving up time with his family in order to bring them back to live with him. He had the most to lose, but the most to gain also.

Originally, I came up for the idea for this story after learning about Ellis Island in school, and doing more research on the process people had to go through to immigrate to the United States.

Q: What was the hardest part of revising your story?

A: The hardest part was finding parts that made sense in my head, but didn't make sense to the reader. I read my story out loud, particularly the conversation between Nicole and the main character. Their dialogue sounded different than intended and once I read it out loud, I realized it needed some revision.

Q: When did you start writing the story?
A: I started writing this story as soon as I heard about the contest, and I'm already working on more stories.

Q: What are your favorite books right now?
A: I love all mystery and adventure books, but right know I really enjoy *The 39 Clues* series most.

Q: What are you writing next?
A: I am thinking of writing a fictional story involving time.

Q: Where is your favorite place to write?
A: I love writing at home the most. It's comfortable and I seem to get more ideas. Usually, I sit at the dining table or in front of a big window, which lets my mind wander and get more creative.

Q: Did you think you were going to change much during your revision?
A: I was pretty confident in my story overall, but I also knew there would be a few key points to make clear for the reader. Revising was a very important part of the process to help get my ideas across.

Q: Have you ever had "writer's block," and, if so, what do you do to get out of it?
A: I've definitely had that before. Usually I'll go outside into fresh air when I'm not making any progress on an idea. Then, when I come inside, I usually have a few more ideas. Sometimes I'll also play with my sister or walk around in the yard.

A Journey to America

by

Sanjay Ravishankar

Ellis Island, Dec 26, 1900, 2:43 pm

Pounding rain soaked my clothes, not to mention my heart. I was outside on a bench, waiting for the results of my citizenship health test. The anxiety, mixed with a high-strung feeling, was boiling inside of me. The piece of bread in my pocket I had been saving for four days was as hard as rock. My teeth crunched on the crust as I checked my watch. It had been thirty-nine minutes since the doctors sent me out. We'd docked on Ellis Island earlier today. It was Dec 26, 1900, 2:43 pm, and the day after Christmas. I was so excited when we docked. My excitement multiplied when I saw all the Christmas decorations, as beautiful as peacocks. It was the first time my family and I were away from our home country, Peru, South America. I was with my family, but now my family is gone . . . *Don't think about that, Don't think about that, DON'T THINK ABOUT THAT!* Yet I kept my family in mind. I still wandered to a flashback, a sad flashback . . .

Port of Callao, Peru, Jun 19, 1900, 7:16 am

I was at the port of Callao, with my family, looking at the brand-new clean ship, named GREAT TRIPS.

"I really wish we could board that ship," cried my daughter, Andrea. My son, Sebastian, was at the shop with his mom, Nicolle. Who knows what they were buying. When I saw them walking out, they had a bag full of snacks. I started waving my hand to get their attention. A deafening ship's horn surprised me. As I turned around, I saw that another ship was here. The ship was so tawny, with the bow rusted. I could only make out STO P I T, or STOP IT! I realized we had to board that old, rusty ship.

When we boarded the ship, we were escorted towards the steerage area. The ship smelled like rotten . . . everything! By the next few days, the port of Peru slowly faded away as I saw nothing but the blue waves of the clear liquid. Steerage was cramped with a dirty floor and a small café that only served bread. The ride was putrid and unpleasant. Seasickness made it smell like dirty socks worn for a month mixed with two-month-old stale milk. The trip took about six months.

The Port of Ellis Island, Dec 26, 1900, 8:09 am

We reached the cold port of Ellis Island, the immigration center. When we went inside the huge, warehouse-like structure, my heart felt like it was boiling in a mixture of nervousness and excitement.

We might be able to enter America! We will be in the land of the free and the home of the brave!

My thoughts were interrupted by a rather old man, probably in his fifties or sixties.

"EXCUSE ME!" he yelled. "Watch where you're going." The old man continued chasing after his own kid.

When we came to the front of the queue, about two to three hours later, I was so nervous, I felt like a piece of cheese next to a hungry rat. We set our leather baggage on the long black counter.

The officers checked our belongings, enough intis to make roughly 2.73 U.S. dollars, and papers/documents confirming our jobs back in Peru. The guard asked us all kinds of questions.

"What is the purpose of your visit?"

"We came here to get a job and for a better living."

"Did anyone else travel with you?"

"No, it's just us four."

When we answered all the questions, we were all set to go to the next test area.

On the walk to the Great Hall, where our next test was to take place, we had to climb a giant staircase. I was flabbergasted. It was probably the biggest set of steps I had ever seen.

"How tall is this?" I asked.

The guard replied, "About a hundred and three feet."

"Do we have to climb these humongous stairs?" Andrea whispered to Nicolle .

She whispered back, "Of course, if you want to enter America."

Up, up we went, but on the 79th stair, Sebastian peeked forward to see how many more stairs were left. That's when everything happened at once. Sebastian hit his chin on the railing. By the time I turned around,

Andrea jumped backward to save him. When Jennifer took one step down, both the children rolled down the stairs in a human snowball, and the guards caught them.

"You two have to return to the ship."

"But why?" I found myself asking.

"Because your children slipped!" he angrily told me.

From the top of the stairs, I watched my family head back to the ship, but then an officer stopped them. He told Nicolle something, and then they headed to a different exit.

I asked the guard, "Why are they going through the other way?"

"Because you will see them again in the kissing post," he replied.

A light bulb rang in my head. I can see them again! I can see them again! I can see them again!

As I jogged down the stairs toward the kissing post, I noticed the famous Statue of Liberty. From this angle, it had a halo on the torch, which made it seem like the torch was a real flame. Of course, that was just my imagination. When I reached the bottom, my family was nowhere in sight.

I asked the officer standing next to me. He said it would take longer since we were in steerage. Soon enough, my family came walking out the door, so I almost ran to them.

"Nicolle, I should stay with you three. I don't care if we don't get money."

"No."

"Listen to me; I need to stay with you. If we are lucky, I will get admitted in the same woodcutter job," I said.

"I know this is hard and unplanned. But you must stay in

America for us."

I said, "I will not go without my family."

"Go anyway. Keep in touch," Nicolle was saying as a guard pulled them away.

"You people have to board the ship."

The hard tone of the officer's voice made me think twice before asking my next question, but I did, anyway. "Can't we just have five more minutes?"

"No, you can't," said the officer, raising his tone. "If the ship leaves too early, we will keep you here in America, but since they don't have proper freedom, they will roam around here, and we will keep an eye on them. Do you want that to happen?"

"No," I whispered quietly.

I entered the Great Hall and took my next test. The doctors had to see if I was healthy enough to go into America. This was the most important test, if you ask me. The doctors were very strict. People on the boat told stories about how you have to get a 74 or above to pass. Some guy got a 73.981, and they didn't let him pass.

When they examined my results, they had a weird look on their faces.

"What happened?" I asked them.

The doctors replied, nervously, "You have a 90 percent chance you won't make in." That was bad news.

I shambled out of the testing center toward the big metal gates separating me from my dream of entering America.

The officers guarding the door asked me gruffly, "What are you

doing here?"

"I am waiting for my results in my health test," I answered. They let me go. I went to the nearest bench. Just when I sat down, rain started to fall.

"Some coincidence," I muttered as the rain fell even harder. I just sat there, waiting.

I gave a once-over at my watch. It was 3:06 pm. I was about to get up and leave when I heard the doors open.

"Did I pass?" I asked nervously.

The doctors answered, "Well, you see . . . um . . . you barely passed."

"Uh-huh, tell me more," I told, excitedly.

The nurse first hesitated, then finally replied, "You were supposed to get a 74 or above to exceed, and you got a 74.38."

"Wow." I was relieved by my health score. *Now I can live a better life, with a better job, and not have scars all over my hand! My family can also live a great life*! The old job was in the forest. The new job I am taking is most likely going to have better tools than an old axe, and maybe be in a less populated forest. In Peru, animals scratched me all over.

Rochester, New York, Dec 13, 1901, 1:20 pm

After a year with a decent job in America, something was lacking. With enough money to provide for my family, the fact they were not with me left a vacant spot in my heart, like a broken piece in a puzzle.

I missed my home, and my family, so I started packing up. I decided to make my way back to Peru, even though I knew I would end up in the same woodcutter job with less salary and poor labor conditions. I didn't care. All I wanted was to be with my family. I realized now that, without them, there was no point in having a good salary.

Leaving America was my toughest choice of my whole life. If my family came to America, life would be perfect, but they hadn't been in contact for the past two to three months, and I was worried about them. I finished up my packing, and an hour later, I was at the harbor waiting for my boat.

Meanwhile, on Dec 13, 1901 3:11 pm, "Luxury R Us" was hitting New York Harbor . . .

"Mommy, are we there yet?" asked Andrea.

Nicolle replied, "Not yet, Andrea."

Sebastian also waited impatiently to see everything. "I want to see Dad," he mumbled.

Andrea agreed, way too hyper. "I can't wait to see our new home," Andrea said quickly.

After half an hour, Luxury R Us stopped at the port with a huge blast of its air horn.

Ellis Island, Dec 13, 1901, 3:16 pm

A loud blare made me almost slip off the wet bench.

Is that my ride back home?

When I glanced above the roof, people piled out of steerage.

Oh, whatever.

Then, I noticed three familiar faces. Could it be? Yes, it was! My family had disembarked out of that ship! Was it a dream, or a miracle?!

I ran around my bench in happiness! Even with the excitement, tension ran through my nerves. Could they pass this time?

I sat quietly for nearly two hours, and then Andrea and Sebastian sprinted towards me, hugging me with emotion, and having tears of joy. Nicolle was jogging out of the Great Hall with their luggage, and then we walked to the home I'd made for us with work I'd done in the past year.

Finally, my family is with me in the land of the free, and the home of the brave.

Rochester, New York, Jul 09, 1903, 1:23 pm

Our lives are happier in America. I learned the value of family over money. Nothing can replace the feeling of home, sparkling with love, brightened with smiles, and secured with hugs.

I often remember the quote: "Family is not an important thing. It is everything!"

It is true.

Streamlining the Language

Dear Reader,

When I first read Mito's poem, "A Letter to Waka-sensei," I could feel the love and respect in Mito's words and the way that she had structured the poem. Already, this work was a touching tribute to her dance teacher.

Like most great poems, Mito's work was full of tension—between what the speaker (the narrator) of the poem knows will happen to Waka-sensei and the innocence of the young girl character in the poem who does not know yet what will happen to Waka-sensei: "I thought you had a fever / . . . Why were you crying?" As a reader, I find this tension very moving.

The existing structure of this poem was also a wise choice, with each stanza beginning at a different point in time: "At four," "At eight," "At nine." Jumping through big gaps in time, Mito was able to show the young girl character in the poem growing up: becoming less innocent, but wise and strong through the experience of losing her important mentor.

Whenever a poem succeeds in these zoomed-out "big picture" areas—the concept, structure, tone, etc.—I like to zoom back in to the teensiest details, looking at each word one by one and wondering why it deserves to be in the poem. I call this "streamlining the language."

Many of Mito's lines were crisp and precise ("I never wore that kimono," "Your head tilted like a turtle's neck," "Now I saw the beauty in the dance."). Others were more conversational; many of them began with "And" and "So" like casual spoken language, and some lines had extra words we didn't need (like "attached" in "with a small wooden dance stage **attached**").

To streamline is to make something smooth and sleek. With a poem that already has a smooth grace and elegance to it, the best revision experiment is to shave away any words that feel repetitive or extraneous. You can also experiment with replacing certain words with more specific words. For example, how does it feel to change "I wrote another letter to you" to "I wrote a **final** letter to you" or even "I wrote a final letter"?

You can think of your existing poem as a sculpture carved out of marble. Are there any small areas where your sculpture still looks rough? You don't need a chisel here. Try a little sandpaper.

Happy revising,
Sarah Lyn Rogers

Sarah Lyn Rogers has worked with Society of Young Inklings since 2012, as an intern, writing mentor, copyeditor, layout designer, and as the Editorial Director for the Your Name in Ink publishing program. She is a Pushcart-nominated writer, the former Fiction Editor of *The Rumpus*, and the author of *Inevitable What*, a poetry chapbook on magic and rituals. A San Francisco Bay Area native, Sarah moved this summer to New York City to be even more tangled up in the world of writing and publishing.

Mito Funatsu

Mito is an eighth grader at Saint Andrew's Episcopal School. She likes to write, ride horses, and play the violin. She was born in Japan and came to the United States when she was nine. She started writing her own stories in a notebook at around the age of five, and has been writing in many genres since then.

Sarah Lyn Rogers: How long have you been writing?
Mito Funatsu: When I was four or five, my mom got me a notebook and I instantly started writing stories. I was inspired by picture books that I read in preschool—the teachers read a lot to us. I started creating my own stories, like bears using magic to get honey.

Q: And how long have you been writing poetry?
A: Since second grade when I was first introduced to poems—in Japanese, actually. Then I made a poem collection and showed it to my friends and family. When I first came here, I didn't start writing poetry because English was still hard for me. Then I had a poetry assignment in seventh grade and realized my love for poems no matter the language. This one was also a school assignment—my teacher said it was very good and I should submit it somewhere.

Q: What is your favorite genre to write, and what kinds of things do you like to write most?

A: I write in a lot of genres; I don't really have a favorite. I like fiction in general. I love describing in detail using many descriptive words. With fiction, I can create my own world and use as much description as I want.

Q: Who are your favorite authors and/or favorite books?

A: I don't have a favorite author, but I've read several books by Laurie Halse Anderson. I think she is an amazing historical fiction writer. I read a lot of historic and scientific fiction. I know a lot of people would say Harry Potter, but I've actually never read Harry Potter. I can't really immerse myself in fantasy books.

Q: What useful thing did you learn during this editing process?

A: I learned a lot of things, but I learned that a poem doesn't really have one way of writing it. It's more like art and how you express yourself. A poem is about how it sounds, and how it looks, too. That was pretty interesting. Learning about streamlining the language was very helpful–making sure that every word has a reason to be in my poem.

Q: What are you writing next?

A: Right now I'm starting a scientific fiction story. It's going to be a short story about virtual reality. I hear a lot about virtual reality these days and I've tried many virtual reality experiences at museums. Then I wondered, "What if these got so real that people got confused?"

A Letter to Waka-sensei

by

Mito Funatsu

When my chubby baby cheeks started to deflate,
I dreamed of a dancer dressed in a kimono.
So I took slow tiny steps into the room,
A room with a small wooden dance stage.
You sat there smiling,
I hid behind my mother's back.
You talked to my parents, smiling and laughing.

At four, I started taking lessons from you.
I followed you around on the stage,
That was my lesson.
I never wore that kimono,
How could I have found joy in the slow, "beautiful" moves?
Your head tilted like a turtle's neck, and your feet slid inwards,
While I yawned at your right hand that raised the fan.

At eight, a bandana fully covered your head,
But your smile still lingered on your face.

Now I saw the beauty in the dance,
I was walking closer to my dream.
My mother told me to write a get well card,
I thought you had a fever.
I handed it to you shyly,
Why were you crying?

At nine, I flew overseas to America.
I wrote a final letter to you,
Because I knew this time.
You gave me a call,
I froze at your tears I felt from miles away.
Nothing came out of my mouth,
Not even a simple thank you.
When I got another call,
This time from your wife,
Tears streamed down my face for the first time.

Your smile never died,
Even when I last saw you on my dream stage wearing a red kimono.
People say I dance like you,
And when I dance I am still mimicking your moves.
Your family says I was like your daughter to you,
Now I cannot thank you enough.
When I fly back to Tokyo next time,
Please let me greet you,
On the stage you taught me what my life is now.

Heart of the Story through Specificity

Tasslyn Magnusson mentored Amann Mahajan through a revision that used specific details to emphasize the message in her story, "A Tidbit of Magic."

Dear Reader,

Finding the heart of the story—that's a challenge! How do you know exactly what your story is about? Sometimes it's just there from the beginning and sometimes your characters have to tell you a little bit more and you've got to follow them a little further to understand your heart. When Amann and I met, we decided to do a lot of different kinds of brainstorming around showing her story—not just telling her story.

We started with verbs. Verbs and their tenses are a way a writer can shape what the reader will feel. Amann read her story and thought about this question: how close to the action do I want the reader to feel? We brainstormed as many verbs as possible, thinking about past tense and present tense. In her first draft, Amann wrote: "The old lady pats my cheek. Without knowing it, either, the cookie has disappeared down my throat." That first sentence is in present active tense. The reader is right there. We can see the old lady pat the cheek. We feel connected and maybe even like we are in the scene. I asked Amann to look at the second sentence and asked her what would happen if she wrote it in present tense, too. "Without even knowing it, the cookie disappears down my throat." I can almost feel a cookie slipping down my throat. Active present verbs bring your reader closer to the scene—closer to the heart of the story.

Next, Amann and I talked about a phrase that is very familiar to writers: show me, don't tell me. In her draft, Amann wrote: "The house at the corner smells smoky and sharp." This is a terrific example of showing the reader. I learn a lot. I know how the character feels—maybe apprehensive or like danger is near, and the "sharp" tells me it could be really quick. I know, as your reader, to pay attention!

Amann allowed herself to really play with her words and explore all of the possible verbs she could imagine. She didn't use them all. But they helped her have lots of ideas to pick from and to feel excited by revision—and not worried. A lot of times, revision can worry people because we are afraid of making a mistake. When you brainstorm words, you can get excited about the possibilities. Amann did a great job. Her face lit up when I asked her what she liked best about revision: "Thinking about everything I could do!"

All of these techniques helped Amann make her story strong and specific. What I was most impressed by, however, was her willingness to write new scenes that were extra sad but helped the reader see the heart of the story. It's always challenging to write about sad things. But when Amann wrote a new scene that showed the reader about how her character was sad, it made the love the main character finds in the end with Grandma all the more powerful. She truly found the heart of her story.

Congratulations, Amann! Thank you for sharing your work!

Tasslyn Magnusson

As a fourth grader, Tasslyn Magnusson once tried to read her school library from A to Z, backwards. She got stuck on P.L. Travers and *Mary Poppins* and has been reading anything and everything since. When she's not writing her poetry or working on her middle grade novels, she's reading fan fiction written by her teens and trading book recommendations with their friends. Tasslyn received her MFA in Writing for Children and Young Adults from Hamline University in January 2017. She has had several poems published and won the 2017 Room Magazine Poetry Prize.

Amann Mahajan

Amann is a sixth grader who lives in Stanford, California. She loves to read and write, and do math and astronomy. She is considering becoming an astrophysicist when she grows up. Amann enjoys music and plays the piano and flute, and sings. She has a ten-year-old brother named Kabir. He is very sweet (well, as sweet as younger siblings can get). Amann goes to Terman Middle School (which will be Ellen Fletcher Middle School next year), and enjoys learning there. She is excited to be in the *Inklings Book* again, since she was in it in 2014. Amann has also won a playwriting contest. She wrote this story for her grandmother, Sujaya, who has Alzheimer's disease.

Tasslyn Magnusson: What is your favorite book?
Amann Mahajan: I like to read—a lot! I don't have a favorite, but right now I'm reading *Bud, Not Buddy*. I found it in my classroom library and it looked good, so I borrowed it from my teacher. I also like Agatha Christie.

Q: Why do you enjoy writing?
A: Because it's a way to put the way you're feeling into words or the characters can feel what you're feeling. It can be a magical experience or be whatever you want it to be.

Q: What is your favorite thing to write?
A: Fantasy. I write mostly fantasy.

Q: Where do you like to write?
A: At a table. Any desk or table. In the kitchen. On the kitchen table.

Q: When did you start writing?

A: Probably when I was five. I wrote these little stories. My second grade teacher had us write short stories and share them with the class. I liked that.

Q: What changed when you revised "A Tidbit of Magic"?

A: I added more scenes with action instead of just describing; I showed a scene where they told a story instead of just saying they told a story.

Q: You tried a lot of techniques–drawing action in scenes, looking for active verbs. What was your favorite revision activity?

A: Probably showing, not telling–adding action to scenes, making characters do things.

Q: What advice do you have for Inklings who might not like to revise?

A: Sometimes you feel like you don't have to revise. Play around with it. Just ask yourself: Would it sound better if I did this or this? Or change the ending? Just play around with it! If you have writer's block, you could draw ideas–like I wasn't sure how to resolve the conflict in my story. I took a walk and tried to draw the ways to resolve the conflict and talked with my mom about my ideas.

Q: Where do your story ideas come from?

A: Sometimes they come from real life experiences or something or someone or a book you read or just your imagination–if you see something, and your mind starts wondering and you start telling yourself a story.

Q: What are you going to write next?

A: I was working on a story about this place where music is being controlled and there was no joy in it and a person travels through the villages and brings the music for everyone to enjoy.

A Tidbit of Magic

by

Amann Mahajan

August 3rd, 1999

Every day after school, I pass by the house on the corner of Willow and Fandango. It seems to me that it was built before the others on the block, for it seems old fashioned; it looks rickety and old, and you can see a staircase through the windows that leans precariously to one side. The yellow paint is cracked and crumbly on the outside, and you can see the plaster sticking out from underneath.

Most of the time, though, the smells coming from the house make up for its appearance. Usually there's a sharp, cinnamon-like fragrance wafting from it: a hint of lemon, a tang of citrus. The smell is magical, almost; every day, it fills me with a kind of joy, a kind of hopefulness tinged with a dab of sorrow. All of those emotions in a single heartbeat.

Neighbors say that the old lady is senile, that she stays shut up in that old house all day. I catch glimpses of her: frizzy gray hair, startlingly hazel-hued eyes framed by big square glasses, sunken-in

cheeks. Oh, those eyes—the sorrow in them, the longing in them. The feelings that are hinted in those smells that emanate from that house.

Those moments, when I smell those smells, are the good moments in my day. At home, it's just me, Sissy, and Father; he constantly broods on the past and worries about bills. Ever since Mother left to New York, he has been different. Sadder. Angrier. He neglects us; he yells at us, too, sometimes. There are rare moments when he sighs and shows small gestures of affection. I usually make the meals for me and Sissy. Father truly is a mess.

Sissy, though, is radiant, a miniature star lighting up our shabby home. Every day, I tell her a story in our small room at bedtime, no matter whether my day has been worse than usual or moderately good. It is our routine. Most of the time, I tell her a fairy tale of my own creation. I tell her tales of enchantresses, dragons, knights, and powerful queens. Then I give her a small smile, tuck her in, and give her a light kiss on her forehead.

At school, I remain quiet. I observe. Today, Donald Curtz bullied people—a regular thing. I sat on a bench and ate my expired bagel, slumping down on the bench and pulling my hood up over my head. And Donald passed right by me. Being nonexistent has its benefits.

My life is based on routine, a never-ending pattern of monotony, plodding forward each day. Sometimes, when the sun comes out in these parts, I remember Mother. How she broke the pattern each day, how she took us somewhere new every day. Around here, though, sun is scarce. When I do see it, I get sunburns.

August 5th

Sissy is sick. Very sick. I sit by her, and she allows only me to hold her. Father mutters constantly about medical bills. His eyes are sunken and they have deep rings underneath. He is a sad man. A sad man.

The smells coming from the house on the corner of Willow and Fandango are sweeter by the day. Cinnamon. It's always cinnamon, or at least a hint of it braided within the other scents. She uses a walking stick now. Her house continues to become more unstable by the day. I wonder why she never fixes it. She seems to be in a world of her own.

August 21st

Sissy is in the hospital now. Father screamed at my mother's picture today, asking her why she left him to go to New York "with all of… *this* to take care of." The bills. The house. Us. He doesn't like to look at us because we remind him of her.

I sit with Sissy in all of my free time, watching her pale, gaunt face and ragged breathing. Her body feels as weightless as a rag doll. I stroke her hair and tell her stories, my mind wandering to the old lady and her concoctions and her yellow house. Today, I tell Sissy a tale that reminds me of her.

"Once upon a time," I begin, "there was—"

"Once upon a time!" Sissy squeals, as always. "My favorite beginning!"

I smile. "Once upon a time," I continue, "there was an old lady who made potions."

"Like a witch," Sissy interrupts, eagerly.

I nod, smiling. "Like a witch. Every day she made potions to cure people of their sadness and sickness. Everyone in her village was happy."

I look down at Sissy and trace her eyebrows. "There was one family in the kingdom, the King's servants, who didn't have enough money to travel to the witch. In that family, a little girl was sick."

"Like me?" inquires Sissy.

I smile weakly. "Like you. So the little girl's brother traveled to the witch to collect the potion. He fought evil monsters and wicked sorcerers with his sword made of silver. He retrieved the potion."

"What does 'retrieved' mean?" asks Sissy.

"To bring back," I reply. "So this witch gave him the potion. It smelled like cinnamon."

"My favorite!" Sissy squeals.

"But," I continue gravely, "the King said that the little girl could not have the potion because the King would have to pay for it."

"Oh no!" Sissy gasps.

"Oh yes," I say. "So the little girl and her brother escaped to the hills and made a home there, with all the animals. The little girl drank the potion, and she became better again. The end."

I look down at Sissy. She is breathing peacefully, almost asleep. A small smile is on her lips. I lean down and tuck her in, feeling sadder and wiser than I ever have felt. Then, as always, I plant a light kiss on her forehead. I cherish every moment with my beautiful, wise, enthusiastic, and loving sister. But I don't know how much time she has left.

December 5th

Sissy is gone. I miss her already.

Last night, I told her about a brother and a sister both escaping to a palace in the sky. Little did I know that the brother would be left behind.

December 6th

Father is broken now. Mentally. Emotionally.

I never thought he loved Sissy. Maybe he did. Either way, there's the medical bill. Overall, there is a large number with more than one zero after it, to put it simply.

I think I knew all along what would have to happen if Sissy died. The medical bill would exhaust most of our small supply of money. So, when Father tells me, today, that he can no longer support both of us, and that I must leave the house, it does not come as too much of a surprise.

I will remember this moment, always. The small brown door with the peeling paint, and Father's face behind it, as I board my bike to leave. Where to? Who knows? I am hollow.

Father's face is a puzzle. Can I see grief? Maybe. Anger? Perhaps. Love?

That I cannot see, not anymore.

I suppose I lost my father a long time ago. I lost that loving, hopeful man when I lost my mother.

I take one last look at the scene, wondering if it could have been any different. Then I hitch up my bike, and, still looking, throw one leg over the seat.

Then I leave. I don't look back.

It is a bitterly cold late autumn day. I decide to bike around until I find somewhere I can stay temporarily. I cycle past Willow and Fandango. The house at the corner smells smoky and sharp. I hear a scream.

I leave my bike and open the door, which is unlocked. The old lady is on the floor.

"Are you all right?" I ask, helping her up.

She looks at me, no comprehension in her eyes. She tilts her head. She points to me, then puckers her eyebrows.

She grabs my hand, suddenly. She pulls me to the kitchen of her house, which is just as dirty and disheveled as the rest of the house. She opens the oven.

Six black, burnt cookies lie on the tray. Shaking her head, she throws them out. She walks out to the back of her house, motioning for me to follow. She points to a tree in her backyard. It almost seems to glow. The leaves are green, and bright pink berries grow on it. She reaches a trembling hand to pick some. Unable to reach any, she sighs.

I reach upward and grab a bunch of berries. At once, my hand feels warm, very warm. A surge of joy races through me. I hand the berries to the old lady, who beams. She pats my cheek affectionately and proceeds inside. She motions for me to follow.

She grabs a bunch of ingredients, all of them simple–butter, sugar, flour–and then adds the bright berries. At once, the dough turns bright pink.

She sticks the concoction into the oven and sets the temperature to 400 degrees.

"For cookies?" I say disbelievingly. "Isn't it, like, 350 or something?"

She shakes her head.

While the cookies bake, she leads me up the rickety stairs into a room. It is littered with papers, and papers adorn the walls as well. She shows me one.

Laura Wandaberry, it says. She points to herself.

"Mrs. Wandaberry?"

She nods, and gives me a faint smile. It doesn't reach her eyes, though. There is a dimple on her left cheek.

She runs her hand over a photograph on the wall. It is one of a man in a uniform. It is faded, and black and white. The man has a wide smile and seems to be greeting a friend heartily. She points to a name underneath.

"Mr. Wandaberry?" I say, slowly. "Where is he?"

Her eyes darken. I can see the sorrow sweep through them once again. I am about to apologize when I smell the smell.

It is the same smell that I smell every day. The same sharp, tangy smell of cinnamon, sweet and spicy and sad at the same time. She—I mean Mrs. Wandaberry—takes my hand and leads me downstairs. She opens the oven, and the smell washes over me. It reminds me of all the times that I've been happy—with Sissy, with Mother, in our old home.

The cookies are bright pink, like the dough. She offers the tray to me, and I take one, hesitantly. Who knows what's in those berries?

I bite into the cookie. It is soft, and it tastes like cinnamon and happiness mixed together. Sweet, spicy, tangy, happy, sorrowful.

Without realizing it, I am crying. From joy. From sorrow. From everything.

The old lady pats my cheek. Without realizing it, either, the cookie disappears down my throat.

"There must be some kind of magic in those cookies," I say to her, although I now know that she is mute and cannot answer.

She nods.

"A secret ingredient?"

She nods again. She puts up the number three.

"Three of them?"

She nods for a third time.

"What are they?"

She gives me a lopsided smile. A dimple forms in her left cheek. This time, the smile reaches her eyes.

"Um," I say. I swallow. Something's compelling me to do this. "Can I stay with you?"

She smiles at me.

"I take that as a yes?"

She winks at me, then nods. I smile back, although I feel an ache in the left side of my chest.

December 9th

I have been staying with Mrs. Wandaberry for three days now. I trust her, and she trusts me. I call her Grandma. By stringing together newspaper clippings and photographs, she has told me about her past. Her whole body is weighted down by her sorrow. I think she bakes the cookies to filter it out. She bakes them, but never eats them.

Her husband was a soldier in World War II. He died fighting

the Nazis, and so she was left all alone. Her father had enlisted, too, and he had died as well. Her mother had left her as well when she was very little. She knew heartbreak. She *was* heartbreak.

I look at her frail, broken body often. I think she lives in the past. She lives in those years of sorrow and death. I try to bring her back.

"Grandma," I beg. "Please. I know I have no idea what you've been through, but I *do* have an inkling. I lost my sister. You lost your whole family. There is a difference, I know. But if those cookies helped me, they will help you. You need them. You hear me, Grandma?" I shake her hands, trying to be gentle but not succeeding entirely.

She looks at me. Her face, though wrinkled, is unblemished: It is as if she has not seen the sun in a long time.

She shakes her head.

December 19ᵗʰ

We are preparing for Christmas. I love Grandma. She loves me, too. On those precious days when the sun comes out, I no longer get sunburns. Instead, Grandma takes me out, sometimes to Golfland, sometimes to get sweet, cold, creamy ice cream, sometimes to eat exotic foods downtown. And we smile and exchange thoughts and wishes and happy memories.

Now, as I said, it is almost Christmas. I have gone out and bought us a tree. The sharp air refreshes my memory. I remember Sissy. Father. Mother. I block my mind from it all. They were in the past. I am here now. Still. I have not told a single story since Sissy died. Not one.

It hurts too much to think about them. Grandma helps me through my sorrow. I help her through hers.

Some days, I hold her hands in mine, and she holds my hands in hers. We just sit there, mutely, in a kind of vigil for our lost loved ones. Then she wraps her arms around me like she will never let go. I comfort her, and she comforts me, all without a single word.

We work together, Grandma making the cookies and me making decorations. The old yellow house has never been more productive. The smell of the magical cookies, spicy, sweet, happy and sad, emanates from the house constantly.

December 20ᵗʰ

Grandma is in the hospital.

She is almost panting, and I can hear a rattle in every breath. She fainted for the first time since I met her. The doctors have been watching over her constantly. They say that she had a stroke.

I sit by her day and night.

I remember Sissy.

In the bottom of my heart, I know what will help her: the cookies, cinnamon-like, sweet, spicy, citrusy, tangy, sad, happy, magical.

But, in the bottom of my heart, I know that she will never eat them. She doesn't want to remember. She doesn't want to forget, either. She wants to lock it away, keep it inside her, forever. Only her eyes betray that hunger for happiness.

And maybe it isn't just that.

I have not told a single story since Sissy died. I have not embraced it. I am also still living in the past, with the sorrow. Stories made Sissy happy. I don't know if they will make Grandma happy, too.

Besides. I can't.

So we are both here, Grandma an invalid, me an indecisive

young boy, waiting for magical construction workers to cement together our broken hearts.

December 21ˢᵗ – 24ᵗʰ

Every day, I sit by her, talking to her, stroking her hand, tracing her eyebrows. Every day, I remember what happened to Sissy. Every day, I ache.

We *are* keeping the truth away from ourselves.

But I cannot go on like *this* one day longer, either. I just cannot. And I know what I have to do. I come in to Grandma's hospital room, clean and bright, with two things. A story, and a cookie.

"Once upon a time," I begin. I swallow the grief that wells up in me as I utter Sissy's favorite beginning. "Once upon a time, there was a little boy."

I look down at Grandma. I love the moments like this, where we just sit and understand each other. She understands me more than anyone else has, although she has no words to say.

"The little boy had a father and a sister. His sister was his life. His father cared nothing for either of them. He was always wrapped up in memories of his divorced wife and bills."

Grandma cocked her head.

"One day, the sister became sick. Very sick," I continue. "The brother told her stories day and night. She lived on the stories and thin broth. She lived for a very long time on just those two things. But then . . . " I feel a lump the size of a basketball in my throat. "Then she died. The father, overcome by grief, anger, and stress, threw the little boy out of the house."

"The little boy left his house and rode his bicycle to the yellow

house on the corner. The smells there always made him happy. The house smelled like cinnamon and magic, sharp and sweet and spicy and sad. But at the same time, very happy." I look down at Grandma again. By now, I can barely see the essence of her, clinging onto every word.

"The boy saved the old lady inside the house. They became a family. The boy helped the old lady, and the old lady helped the boy." I sigh. "The old lady knew heartbreak. She *was* heartbreak. Her family was gone, years ago, killed in a war of strife and pain. But she lived in the past. She could not face the truth of the present, where she was now, where she lived now. She never ate any of the magical cookies she made. And when she got sick, the little boy told her a story." I look at her with a slight smile on my lips. "This one."

I reach my hand into my pocket and take out a bright pink cookie. "I know the secret ingredients now," I whisper. "The magical berries. Sorrow. Happiness. Memories."

She nods, almost wistfully. And, with a wise bow of her head, as if she knew this was going to happen all along, she accepts the cookie.

She bites.

I can see the memories, the sorrow, the happiness, the magic, flow through her. Just like me, silent tears roll down her cheeks. And just like me, she finishes the cookie before she knows what's happening.

"I told you it would help," I scold, shakily. "It did."

Grandma smiles. The blood rushes back into her cheeks, filling her with a beautiful happiness I have never seen in her before. I can see the sorrow disappear from her eyes.

The doctors come in, and check her over. "A miracle," they mutter. "How could she have been cured so quickly?"

"It could have been magic," I say, a quirky smile playing on my lips. "And stories."

The doctors frown at me. "You can take her home, boy," one says. "And that tosh—magic and all—I would stay away from that."

"Yes, sir," I say, too happy to disagree. I give Grandma's hand a little squeeze. "I'll take her home now."

So I did.

December 25th

This has been the happiest Christmas that I remember. Grandma and I have gotten over the past. We are here, now, and we are not alone anymore. The cookies she shares with everyone, but the magic only we know. And we have added to that magic.

Do you want to know the secret ingredient we have added?

I think you already know.

It's love.

CODA

Once upon a time, there was a boy who was lost. There was a frail old lady who was lost. And they found each other.

They were full of memories and pain. They never knew what a happy ending was, until it happened.

And all because of a story and a cookie, and a tidbit of magic.

Dialogue to Build Clarity

Jenn Castro helped Jeein Choi through a revision using dialogue to explain the details of the plot in her story, "Just May."

Dear Reader,

Sometimes a story is so good, it's hard to find places to make it even better. "Just May" by Jeein Choi is one such story. Jeein has the art of creating realistic scenes showing middle schoolers' angst and worries about friendship. She's also skilled at pairing those scenes with realistic dialogue.

Because Jeein was so adept at showing the middle school students' worries and angst, we wondered if she might be able to further heighten the intensity of May's feelings of rejection from her former best friend by writing another dialogue scene where May is seeking Wendy using dialogue.

The area chosen for Jeein to strengthen her story was to clarify dialogue. Jeein succeeded here in several examples. She changed dialogue between May and her teacher, to make sure May appeared respectful toward the adult, but also to convey that May felt shamed by her teacher. Jeein used effective dialogue paired with character action to stretch out the tension on the playground between May and Wendy's seeker/sought friendship. Jeein impressed me with how easily she created the new scene in the library to not only add another instance when Wendy deserted May, but also to show Wendy lying to May.

Jeein did the important work that all writers must do in revision. First, she reread her story several times with another person. Next, she became willing to revise! She returned to her story and found the essential place to add that one more dialogue scene. Even though Jeein consulted with me about her changes and the places to put them, she always made the final decisions.

If you're writing a story, you might try Jeein's revision approach. Read over your story with someone else, and look for places you could change. Most of all, like Jeein, find the willingness to alter dialogue, adding a new scene as needed, and include tie-together sentences where necessary!

Like Jeein, you may add only a few more lines of dialogue with a new scene. Letting those changes enliven the tension between your characters can enhance your story and make it more how you want it to be. Like Jeein advises, be willing to revise. You won't be sorry; you'll be happy with the changes!

Have fun revising!
Jenn Castro

Jenn Castro—writer, teacher, and mentor—will probably never stop reading kids' books, especially coming-of-age stories, middle grade chapter books about ordinary young people, and children's picture books. As a writing mentor, Jenn takes joy in helping kids build self-confidence in their writing, especially during revision. When Jenn's not working with young writers, she's leading kids' lit clubs, children's backyard theatre groups, and writing on her website, *jenncastro.com*. A Young Inklings mentor and teacher, Jenn lives in California with her husband and two teenagers.

Jeein Choi

Jeein is in fourth grade at Simonds Elementary School in San José, California. She enjoys reading and writing realistic fiction. When Jeein's not writing, she's watching documentaries, playing tennis, and swimming. For her next project, she wants to write a novel, not a short story!

Jenn Castro: Is it easy for you to write?

Jeein Choi: I read a lot. It's hard to choose a new plot. There are so many books and it seems like I'm copying. I know there must be one new story idea I can find!

Q: How do you feel about revision?

A: At first when my mom said, "Write whole new sections," I said, "No! No! No!"

Q: What changed for you when you added an additional paragraph about Wendy and May?

A: After I added the new section, it was refreshing. I could see the benefits I didn't notice before my mentor pointed them out!

Q: What advice do you have for Inklings who don't like revision very much?

A: Revision makes the story better. If you want the best story, revise and it will be satisfying and worthwhile in the end.

Q: Do you like to read? When did you start writing?

A: When I lived in Korea, I didn't like reading because we read only nonfiction. When I moved to America in second grade, I started reading realistic fiction: *Out of My Mind* by Sharon Draper, *When You Reach Me* by Rebecca Stead, among others. I started writing after reading realistic fiction.

Q: Why do you enjoy writing? Where do you write?

A: It feels good to write my own stories. I write at home in my free time. I use my dining table and my room.

Q: Do you ever get blocked?

A: Sometimes when I'm at the end of a story and just about to finish, I feel like giving up.

Q: What do you recommend to others who get blocked?

A: Rest!

Q: Are you working on a new story?

A: I am working on another realistic fiction story. I want to write a real novel, not a short story. I wonder how writers write so many words and pages without quitting!

Just May

by

Jeein Choi

Disabilities

"To win the respect of the intelligent people
And the affection of children;
To earn the appreciation of honest critics
And endure the betrayal of false friends;
To appreciate beauty;
To find the best in others;
To leave the world a bit better . . . "

"Are you listening?" a voice asks. Two meaty hands shake my shoulders fiercely. I look up. Everyone is staring at me with contempt or mockery—Mrs. Wanton, her students.

Even Wendy.

She's my best friend.

Mrs. Wanton shakes her head with exasperation.

"May, were you even listening?" Then, she takes out her canary yellow binder, probably writing another note to my parents about my ignorance. "I mean, about the poem we're reading right now. Were you following along?"

"Yes, Miss." I lower my head and stare at Mrs. Wanton's feet.

Mrs. Wanton narrows her eyes and her hand and pen go flying across the paper inside the binder. I think that the yellow color painted on the binder is a bit too effervescent for cranky, strict Mrs. Wanton. Wanton means evil; my dad had once told me. She goes to her poem again and continues to read aloud the words of Ralph Waldo Emerson. But the words can hardly be heard over the noise. I hear what all the students of Mrs. Wanton's class are talking about.

Me.

And it is all bad stuff—hostile whispers and disapproving frowns. Taunting smirks and quiet mocking laughter can be heard like the high-pitched sparrow calls, both loud and ear-piercing. I try to cover my ears without anybody noticing. I just want to block out all the bad stuff. Think about all the good stuff. How people used to praise me. I think about the time I almost burned off my arm. That isn't the best memory I have of the past.

"May!" a voice yells into my ear. Mrs. Wanton glares at me. "Were. You. Listening?"

"Of course!" I defend myself, glaring at her in a way I hope she won't notice.

"We'll talk about this later," Mrs. Wanton warns me, but fortunately, I am saved by the bell.

"Bye, Mrs. Wanton!" I shout over the loud chatter in the hallways and the rummaging and struggling of students in the classroom, trying to put all their books inside their backpacks. "Good day!"

I swing my backpack over my shoulder, and I run out the door. I can feel Mrs. Wanton's eyes boring a hole through my back.

In the hallway, I weave around a group of giggling girls and a band of bully boys like a squirrel in a tree. Meaning I move stealthily.

At least that's what I try to do.

My backpack's normally really light, but today, I have extra books in my bag and the homework Mr. Humbler (or whatever his name was) gave me is weighing a ton. Used to the lightness of my backpack, I trip. It is more of a collapse to the ground in defeat than a trip. Well, that's what I think.

The majority of students turn their back to their lockers and their eyes drop to the ground to stare at me. That's when all the glances of mockery and the whispers of disapproval and derision start, along with the gossiping. And the scorn starts.

It isn't just my burnt arm that makes other people gossip and look towards me with disgust. I am clumsy. And I keep making dumb mistakes.

"What is seven times two?" a teacher asked, and I raised my hand.

"Nine," I announced proudly to the class and they snickered. Even the teacher smirked for a moment.

Yeah, I'm not good at math. I'll try to be.

Plus, I haven't been able to read well. That's basics.

Three things about me and one thing about today

I'm eleven years old. I've never been able to read decently. It's been very hard, obviously. I get cat confused with *fat*! That is a very

personal statement.

I just started at Richmond Middle. It is not in Richmond. I don't even live in Virginia. In fact, I live way west, across the whole country, in California.

I was never popular around here. Now, not even my best friend protects me. Every day, I fight through insults and scorn. I don't tell my mom or dad. I don't want them to know.

Those were the three things about me.

One fact about today is that today's Thursday. I just left my locker.

I spot Wendy. I run towards her, my backpack flying along with me to Wendy.

"Hi, Wendy!" I call to her. She turns around and her sunburst blonde hair sparkles around her face. Sometimes, I think she's way too cool for me. But she's my friend. Wendy waits and she taps her foot impatiently. She's with another girl. I think her name is Kaitlyn. Or is it Katherine?

"Um," I start to speak, eyeing the Kaitlyn-Katherine girl, "can we walk to my house together? I have nothing today. We can, you know, hang out and watch movies and stuff. You know. Do stuff. Can we?"

Wendy opens her mouth, but she stops herself before she starts to speak. She says another thing instead.

"Mayfly, I'm so sorry, but I already have ballet class in thirty minutes, and I gotta get going. Bye! See you tomorrow then, Mayfly!" Wendy shuts her mouth before she can say anything else. "Come on, Kristen," she says to the Kaitlyn-Katherine (oh, so her name is Kristen!) girl.

Wendy drags Kristen behind her and both of them walk away. Wendy doesn't glance at me behind her shoulder. Not even once. She's too busy chatting and gossiping with Kristen.

Mayfly is a horrible nickname.

Sighing, I adjust the position of my backpack behind my back and I turn around and face the door leading outside. I push open the single blue door and outside, I immediately run to the gates. I push open the metal bar gates of Richmond Middle and amble out of the school. Students who push past me speed up in front of me, so they won't walk by my side.

I expect they know how dumb I am.

My house is right across the street. Spotting its blue roof and the familiar light turquoise walls, I race toward it like my dog Cinnamon, chasing the hot pink rubber ball she has known all her life. I open the door and slip inside, just as Mrs. Lindsey's car enters our street, shaking and rattling, unsteadily making its way down the narrow lane.

In my opinion, it is the number one source of global warming: Mrs. Lindsey's car. If you are in her car and look out the back window, all you can see is gray steam that swirls and dances around as if someone blew over a cup of hot cocoa, like dark brown animals dancing and twirling in the air. I don't know how she drives. And I slam the door shut.

Nobody is home yet. Dad's at work across the town and Mom's off volunteering for Kylie's first grade play. She's making part of the stage.

I toss my backpack on the couch on the way to the kitchen. I reach to open the fridge, but I stop abruptly. I catch myself staring at

an old picture with me in it. The picture is pinned to the fridge with a magnet. There is another girl in the picture. She has blonde hair pulled back into a ponytail. She's Wendy. I reach out and remove the magnet and observe the photo.

I remember. We used to be best friends. Now, Wendy has a bunch of other friends, so she doesn't hang out with me a lot. This makes me think back to the situation near the lockers today. I don't get a million things. Why did Wendy ditch me for Kristen? Why is she wearing a shirt that says *"CHAOS IS MY MIDDLE NAME"*? I don't know the answer to that, but I know one thing: I have known Wendy all my life.

And never, ever in her life did she play ballet.

An unexpected encounter at the library

I am on my way to the library to borrow *Bad News for Outlaws* when I catch the sound of a familiar voice. But the streets are crowded with performers as the local play performed tonight. I don't bother to look to see who it is.

I squeeze my way through the crowd and into the library. Inside, I find silence that I never knew existed.

I have just checked out *Bad News for Outlaws* when I turn around to see Wendy and Kristen tiptoeing behind me.

"Wendy! I thought you would be in ballet!" I say to Wendy, and Wendy looks at her feet.

"Come on, there's nothing interesting *here*." Kristen drags Wendy across the line of checkout devices.

"Wait! Wendy!" I interrupt. "Why did you lie to me?"

"You really expect me to hang out with you every second?

Wow, you have *very* high expectations! Can't I hang out with my *other* friends for a *moment*, at least?"

I want to protest, *But you hang out with them more than me now! You talk to me like I'm your burden, not a friend.* But I keep silent.

For a moment, I size up the situation. Then, I ask something foolish.

"Are you my friend?"

"Of course I am!" Wendy defends herself hotly. "What makes you think I'm not?"

"Friends don't lie to each other."

I grab my book and run out of the library.

First time I ever had fried chicken for dinner

The door opens and Dad comes in. I am in the kitchen doing my homework. I am supposed to write an essay about the difference between an asexual animal and a sexual animal. I am supposed to include information about chickens in here, too.

"Hi, Dad," I practically burst out in fake joy. "How was your day?" I give him my usual strained smile. "Ooh, is that chicken I smell?" I add, sniffing the air in curiosity.

"Yep—it's our dinner. Mom said she'll be a bit late, making all these new stages and backdrops for Kylie's big play. I know you like Mom's salad, but you know that I can't cook. I can't even mix fruit and veggies without spilling a bunch," he replies, taking his coat off, the fabric rustling quietly.

"Funny, I'm supposed to write about chickens in my homework," I inform Dad.

He chuckles at that and asks me, "So how was *your* day, m'lady?"

"Just fine," I manage to lie under my stupid fake smile which is maybe too shiny and phony. Dad gives me a look and I lift my chin slightly in defiance. I give him a *What? I'm innocent! So please don't stare at me that way* look.

Dad shakes his head dismissively, "Okay, I'm hungry already. I've had a long day. So, how about that chicken already, May?"

In which things go from fantastic to terrible

"Now who can explain the difference between a member of the eukaryotes and bacteria?" drones the boring voice of Mr. Humbler.

He is not at all humble. And nobody raises their hands. Sighing with exasperation, he looks around the room for any volunteers. Unlike his voice, his glare is not *boring*, but it is shining with malice. Mr. Humbler is glaring at students all around the classroom and is making all of the students feel uncomfortable. I am sitting in the front row. I don't dare raise my hand. Finally, a kid named Jason raises his hand eagerly, letting out a few "Ooh ooh!"s, "I know!"s, and "Pick me!!!!"s.

"Yes?" Mr. Humbler points at Jason, his stubby finger bulging with effort to stop from dropping down to his side.

"A eukaryotic thing is living and a bacteria is nonliving!" Jason practically shouts, his face glowing with pride.

Mr. Humbler glowers at Jason and glares at the rest of his class until we all can see veins standing out on his forehead and until his face turns tomato red ("I guess I was wrong," Jason says timidly), then to the color of dirty red paint, then to a breaking point. Then, he throws up his arms and starts yelling at the ceiling.

"I've had enough of this!" he roars in impatience and fury.

"That's it! I'm quitting!" And he storms out of his classroom and slams the door behind him. It makes an extremely satisfying *crash* as it slams shut.

For a moment, silence falls upon the class and everybody stares at the still-shaking door. We can hear very loud and grumpy footsteps echoing in the hallways outside. The first one to break out of the trance is Ben, the new kid.

"Wahoo!" he yells and jumps up onto his desk, leaps over onto Kristen's desk, then to Wendy's on his way to Jason. When he lands on Jason's desk, everyone else starts congratulating him wildly. Boys start to shout Jason's name. A boy named Oliver promises that by tomorrow, he will have a banner made with perfection and display it in front of the school. I expect he'll get in a lot of trouble for that.

Will Cranberry leans back on his chair and crosses his arms behind his head. A snobby grin dashes across his face.

"*I* knew the answer to *that*," he announces to the class. Everybody rolls their eyes.

Anyway, we get out in the middle of class. It is our last class for the day, so all the boys agree on skipping the next forty-or-so minutes of school and are off to the streets to get some donuts.

Wendy's off to the mall with Shelly. I catch up to her, ready to ask her to take me with her to the library.

"Um, Wendy," I start, but I am interrupted by Wendy who puts her hands at her hips.

"Listen, Mayfly," she says, staring at me dead in the eye, "I've had enough of you begging to hang out with me. *Us*, I mean," she adds, pointing to herself and then at Shelly who nods fiercely, tossing her long brown hair in agreement. I have no idea where this is going,

but I can tell it's not going to go well.

"You know, I'm tired of you tagging along with us," she continues. "After all, the world doesn't revolve around you, May*fly*." She says the last word with contempt, the same tone the rest of Mrs. Wanton's class uses on me. I back away from her. "Oh, by the way, you are useless here. No need to be here. Why don't you just go away for a minute?" If she doesn't say it with disgust, she basically spits out the words. This day has just gone from fantastic to terrible. I can feel tears welling up inside my eyes. I quickly blink once. Those were some mean words. Really mean. I can't believe she said that. I can't believe that *Wendy* said that. The Wendy I have known all my life.

My world is a tree, supported by my family and friends. They are the ground, my base. When a scoop of dirt is removed from the ground, I collapse. The ground all around me has supported me for a long time. But a scoop of dirt has been removed from the ground. That scoop of dirt is Wendy. My world is falling apart.

Without saying a word, I turn my back on Wendy and Shelly and run towards the gates.

Would you please, please stop crying?

I duck behind a pruned tree outside the building, barely able to resist bursting out into thick, heavy sobs before I disappear behind the stout, solid tree. The trimmed branches and leaves block all outside talking and thoughts. I need privacy. I feel wet, round tears slide down my cheeks, dripping onto my shirt. The shirt reads *"Brave."* I don't feel brave. The only reason that keeps me from wailing like a baby who just wet his diaper is because I am near other students and if they find out, I am going to have to face a great deal of embarrassment.

"Would you please, please stop crying?" says an irritating voice. "Crying doesn't help your situation at all." The voice pauses, almost like it was sizing me up and thinking of another lecture to give me. I look up to see who dares to bother me in this kind of situation, when things are getting out of hand for me.

I find that it's Will Cranberry, that obnoxious kid from science class. He crosses his arms and stares down at me (even though he's not even two inches taller than me) like a mother would do to her mischievous kid who dirtied the floor *again*, just after she finished wiping the floor clean.

"*What?* Quit staring at me that way," I say, squeaking indignantly.

"By middle school, you should be already tough because when you go to high school, it's way worse. You shouldn't be crying over this kind of stuff," he says, shaking his head in this aggravating way that makes me lash back.

"So have *you* been to high school?" I challenge. And I add, "Plus, have you ever been *me*?"

He seems taken aback for a fraction of a second, but he recovers very quickly. And then he says in a voice that is comforting and patient, "Listen. Wendy is just stressed about how she doesn't have time for all her friends. She needs to go to the library everyday with Shelly. Then, she has to go to her ballet class with Kristen. Then–" he is interrupted.

I cried out, "Wendy doesn't even *go* to ballet! She was lying to me. It's just an excuse so she can hang out with all her other friends. Friends that don't include me," my voice fails. "She's too busy to hang out with me, I guess," I add bitterly, kicking a cobblestone that was right next to me. It hurts very much.

"Oh . . . "

"Yeah," I say, staring at a branch that stands out from the rest of the trimmed twigs, for it is uneven and it juts out of the clump of leaves. It isn't pruned.

"May, what I'm trying to say is that Wendy . . . You should forgive her. She's been under a lot of pressure lately. 'Kay?"

"I don't think I ever will."

Will is silent. Then he speaks again. "Please. Do it for yourself. For Wendy. She needs you to be her friend."

" . . . "

I hear Will's name being called. He pleads, "Promise that you'll at least consider it."

And I nod. He nods back to me, turns, and walks away.

Just before he is out of hearing, I shout after him, "Will!"

He turns.

"Thanks," I say, "For calling me May," I add.

He nods solemnly. But he knows that the thank you stands for so much more.

Facing Wendy

The recess bell just rang and the whole class is pushing and shoving each other to get out of the classroom and into open air. I breathe deeply as I make my way out of the classroom. Our teacher Mrs. Czech, who is from Czech Republic, let us out two minutes earlier than usual yesterday. Today, she gave us no homework. Not the best teacher in the world from the principal's point of view, but the best in my point of view. I carry my backpack outside and plop it beside me on the picnic benches near the field. I can hear basketballs bouncing in the basketball courts and the tennis rackets clanking down on the blacktop. The sound of chatting students makes me somber. After all, I don't have anyone to associate with now, since I'm not talking to Wendy.

But I'm going to make a friend again today.

Wendy.

I see her on the picnic benches gossiping with Shelly Jackson like squirrels. I bravely walk towards them with fake confident strides. Soon enough, I reach them and face Wendy and Shelly. They are on top of the table and are staring down at me the way two menacing alley cats would watch an innocent mouse searching for food.

"Why are you here?" asks Shelly, glaring at me with obvious disgust. I ignore her and turn to Wendy.

"Listen, Wendy . . . "

"She has nothing to say to you!" Shelly interrupts. "Right, Wendy?

Wendy steals a glance at me. Then, she looks at Shelly. She places her hands on her lap and starts fumbling with her fingers.

"Give her a chance to say why she's here, Shelly," Wendy replies, glancing at me cautiously. She taps her feet against each other and she is sweating slightly through her purple headband. Shelly nods reluctantly. They both gave me looks that say *Go on, and tell us why you're here.*

"Wendy," I start, "I know what happened yesterday. I'm no fool. But what happened yesterday is just stress. You have a lot of friends. It's been hard to be friends, considering you hanging out with Shelly and Kristen and the others. You keep leaving me and I'm not sure if the new you is fit for me." I stop and take a deep breath. "I miss you.

The old you, I mean. I'm your friend—I'll always be. You're my friend. I wish the old you would come back," I plead.

Wendy looks at me, then Shelly—whose eyes are narrowed slits on her face—then back to me.

"Please, come back." I finish.

She stops fumbling with her fingers. I know she is going to make her decision. She smiles, her hair swirled in happy curls. I can see her aquamarine eyes looking at me. Not with hostility like how Shelly glared at me, but how a true friend would see her friend. She jumps down from her place on the table beside Shelly and stands right in front of me.

I smile and hold out my hand.

"Friends?" I ask.

"Friends," Wendy tells me, shaking my hand. Then she adds, "I'm sorry, Mayfly."

"It's okay, as long as you won't do anything like that from now on."

Wendy smiles and for the first time, I notice her shirt. It says "*Happy!*" That seems like the truth.

"Nice shirt," I comment, gesturing to the vibrant T-shirt, which is rimmed with butterflies on the borders.

"Thanks," Wendy says, hugging me.

It feels so good. When I pull out of the hug, I can't see Shelly anywhere. The recess bell rings. My next class is history. Wendy's next class is science.

Just before I say goodbye, Wendy asks, "Do you want to hang out after school? Mom doesn't expect me to come back until five. We've got plenty of time, Mayfly."

I grin brightly. "Yeah," I reply. She smiles and tosses her hair back.

When she is about two meters away from me, I call out, "Wendy!" She turns towards me. There are students around me, ducking in and out around me to get to their next classes. "It's just May, by the way," I say and then wave. She waves, too, and I turn to go to my next class.

Through the busy crowd, I see Will Cranberry. He saw it all. He nods towards me approvingly and disappears into the raging storm of students.

I look up to the sky. It grins down at me and I feel a tingle of excitement. I sling my backpack over my shoulder and make my way to the history classroom. Even though it is another ordinary day coming back from recess to the classroom, it feel like it is an extra special day for me.

Imagery for Meaning

Ernesto Cisneros encouraged Adam Collins to consider the meaning of each image and how it relates to the message of his poem, "Moon."

Dear Reader,

Even the most experienced writer struggles to capture their thoughts, experiences, and dreams with words. Poetry can sometimes be abstract and nonlinear, meaning it does not follow the rules that we are used to. Sometimes, it can draw upon images to help us navigate its meaning. This is what Adam Collins does all so well in his poem, "Moon."

Anyone who has ever gone outside on a full moon understands that, like the sun, the moon can bring forth the light needed for us to navigate ourselves through the darkness (the darkness being our tough moments in life). The early line, "Sound fades away as the moon rises into the sky, coating the world in a golden glow," reminds us that the sun is not the only source of light.

Part of the revision process was helping Adam to visualize each image he created. To do this, Adam illustrated each line, to help him see the poem in terms of images, not words. The value of this exercise is that it helps ensure that his words create the same images for the reader that he intended.

Taking feedback can be extremely challenging at times. Ultimately, it was up to Adam to decide what changes he wanted to make. An author needs to listen to his advisers, but in the end, it is up to him to decide what parts make sense for him and his work. Adam held on to his final message that "nothing is ever hopeless."

Happy writings,
Ernesto Cisneros

Ernesto Cisneros is a veteran English teacher currently serving the colorful city of Santa Ana, California. He holds an English degree from the University of California, Irvine; a teaching credential from California State University, Long Beach; as well as a Masters of Fine Arts in Creative Writing from National University. He likes to read contemporary books with realistic characters and meaningful storylines full of heart. As a writer, he believes in providing today's youth with honest depictions of characters with whom they can identify. He believes the real world is filled with amazing people with diverse backgrounds and perspectives. His work strives to reflect and bring those stories to life. His latest book, *Efrén Divided*, is scheduled for release in 2020 by HarperCollins.

Adam Collins

Currently, Adam is a seventh grader at Woodside Priory School in Portola Valley, California. When he is not playing baseball, he enjoys hanging out with his two brothers and parents—especially if it involves snow skiing. He loves science, mathematics, history, and getting lost in great books. Some favorite vacation memories have been made while on dinosaur treks, on Revolutionary and Civil War battlefields, and while dodging jellyfish in the Atlantic Ocean.

Ernesto Cisneros: When did you begin writing poetry?
Adam Collins: I began to write poetry in third grade, when our teacher assigned a poetry project. If it wasn't for my amazing third grade teacher, I might not have started to write poems on my own time.

Q: How do you come up with your ideas?
A: I come up with my ideas when I am inspired by others or by something that has happened in my life. The deepest poems come from something that has happened to you, something that you can understand and put your feelings and emotions onto paper.

Q: Do you have any favorite poets or poems?
A: My favorite poet is Shel Silverstein because when I was little, my Dad read his poems to me before bed.

Q: You write about the moon serving as a reminder that "nothing is ever hopeless." What should the reader interpret this to mean?

A: I intended for the message of this line to be that no matter how awful things are going, if you lose a family member or someone special to you, that there is always hope. There is always light at the end of the tunnel.

Q: Are you working on any new poems?

A: Currently, I am revising one other poem called "Ode to Baseball."

Moon

by

Adam Collins

The sun disappears behind the mountain.
The air turns frigid.
Sound fades away as the moon rises into the sky, coating the world in
a golden glow.
Like one big fire, bringing a soothing light to the otherwise dark
night sky.
The shadows, long and eerie, stretch across the ground like a finger,
reaching, grasping at the ground.
The moon, a reminder that life is never completely dark.

That nothing is ever hopeless.

Character Detail

Philomena Block advised Anna Birman on a revision to bring characters to life with specific details in her story, "Kai and Gerda," a retelling of the fairy tale "The Snow Queen."

Dear Reader,

One of the biggest ways you can relate to your reader is with your characters. How do you help your reader invest in a main character within the first few pages? How can you add details to make each character a clear image? Anna did such a great job with imagery in the setting of her story. When Anna and I met to revise her story, "Kai and Gerda," a retelling of the fairy tale "The Snow Queen," we decided to expand on character detail to help make each character jump off the page, as well.

Anna's story involves the infamous Snow Queen and other characters from the original Danish tale. We brainstormed to see how Anna's version of the Snow Queen, Kai, Gerda, and the other characters looked in her mind. We noted how Disney's Frozen was most children today's first introduction to "The Snow Queen" and we worked to show how Anna's version of the characters are very different from the movie. I suggested she sketch out the characters to get a whole picture of each character in her mind. She identified descriptive words for each character and worked to integrate them into her story. Anna also integrated character reactions, thoughts, and opinions so we get a better idea of their personality as well. You'll see her final version on the next pages.

In her revision, Anna did two great things that all writers must do. First, she allowed her newly found details to morph her story. Sometimes, when you finish your story, it's scary to allow new ideas to change the scenes. We can be attached to certain details or parts that may no longer serve the story best. A "final draft" can always be added to. Ideas are so precious, but sometimes you need to let older ideas go so that a stronger version of your story can be told.

Next, she trusted herself and her vision. If you are writing a story with familiar components, like something inspired by another story, allow yourself to shine. Anna's retelling of "The Snow Queen" is different from anyone else's because she allowed her life and experience to motivate her own version. I was so impressed with Anna's ability to use imagery and description to paint a picture, while still keeping the story active and moving forward.

If you are writing a story, you might try Anna's revision approach. Take time to imagine your characters. Draw them out. Take a pencil and write as many words as you can that relate or remind you of the character's physical description and personality.

Sprinkle details throughout the action, instead of using a whole paragraph to describe the character. Use the character's dialogue and reactions to tell the reader even more about the character. Take a break. Come back and see what parts of your story might need to be changed or removed to better fit the new details. Trust your vision.

Remember, like Anna, you might end up with some very different sections from your original draft, but you might discover these details and changes make the story so much more complete and engaging for readers.

Happy writing,
Philomena Block

Philomena Block is an actor, writer, and comedian raised in Santa Cruz, California. Philomena holds two bachelor's degrees—one in musical theatre, the other in psychology—and is trained in playwriting, sketch comedy, and improvisation. Philomena has always been drawn to storytelling and loves developing characters onstage and on the page. Philomena worked as a teacher with Society of Young Inklings for two years and is so happy to get to keep supporting young writers with the Inklings Book Contest. When Philomena isn't writing or performing, she works as a marketing professional and loves exploring nature.

Anna Birman

Anna is in seventh grade at Castilleja. She loves to read, write stories and poems, and spend time with her family and friends. Some of her hobbies include tinkering with art supplies and digital tools, performing in musicals, swimming, and most definitely making others laugh. She enjoys traveling, meeting new people, and exploring nature. Fun facts: She loves the funny and lovable *Peanuts* characters and is fluent in Russian!

Philomena Block: How did you feel when you found out you were selected a winner of the Inklings Book Contest?
Anna Birman: I was really excited because my friend, who also entered with me, told me that we had won! I found out from her at school, and that was really exciting. I needed to check my email first before I believed her!

Q: Your story is based on "The Snow Queen." What inspired you to write about this and retell this story?
A: In English class, we were doing a unit on children's books and my teacher told us to write an introduction to a book and I started the prologue. I had done *The Snow Queen*, this musical–I played Gerda when I was six–and I got a lot of images in my head from that. And when I got home, I got really excited about this, so I just kept writing.

Q: What did you first think when you heard we were focusing on character detail?

A: Let me try and remember . . . hmm. I read your notes first and it registered with me that I had focused a lot more on the imagery of the setting than the characters. And I was like, "Oh, yeah!" I kind of had a vague image of the characters and I tried to make it more in focus. I got to imagine more what they were wearing and looked like.

Q: What were some of the ways you decided to add character detail?
A: First of all, I added physical descriptions when we first meet the characters. When we first meet Krakowsky and Lily, I added dialogue in the forest of them bickering. So you kind of got their personalities more. I also added some of Gerda's thoughts of her while they were bickering. And I added more interactions between the characters. So, I added Kai and Gerda playing more together and interacting more together when they saw the Snow Queen.

Q: Do you have a favorite character detail you added? And why?
A: I really love the parts I added when the Snow Queen first came in. And I love the interactions immediately before she came in–where Kai and Gerda are playing their game and when Gerda is asking Kai what he thinks of the snowflakes.

Q: Do you ever feel blocked when you're writing? What do you do?
A: If I don't know what to write, I like to go back to the story and try and write more about other stuff I've already written. Or I add more imagery somewhere. Or kind of like . . . think about my original idea or the characters and add on to them. But if I can't think of anything else to do, I just leave it completely, and then I come back later. Sometimes I have new ideas. And sometimes you get in a "zone," kind of. So if you're out of it, then you might want to take a break, just to let your mind not be as focused.

Kai and Gerda

A Retelling of the Fairy Tale
"The Snow Queen"

by
Anna Birman

Prologue

The stars shone brilliantly onto the glowing faces of two little children, a girl and a boy. Their names were Gerda and Kai. The girl's long chestnut hair was splayed out and her green eyes were sparkling. Staring up into the same stars were Kai's brown eyes, and on the same cement was his tousled dark brown hair. As they lay there peacefully, they made a promise to each other: "I will always protect you and be true to you. If you are ever lost, I will travel across the world to find you." That was their oath of brotherhood.

The Uninvitee

"Kai, Kai, do you want to play before the guests come?" Gerda climbed through the window, right into Kai's apartment. They were like brother and sister and lived in two apartments in two adjacent buildings, but they found that if they stretched out, they could

place the very tip of their toes on the other's windowsill and pull themselves across.

"All right, all right, I'm ready," he yelled across the room, pulling a red vest over his button-down blouse.

You see, today was New Year's Eve, and children's spirits were soaring with the prospect of oranges and sweets as presents and the dancing that usually lasted the entire night through. However, tension was high among the adults as they scurried and whirled around the kitchens preparing the feast, so the children did their best to stay out of their way. Here in Slovakia, New Year's was taken very seriously.

" . . . and the knight jumps onto the dragon's back!" yelled Kai.

"I'm up here, knight!" cried Gerda from on top of the couch.

"I am coming, my princess! The knight stabs the dragon!"

"Don't get crushed, knight!"

"Have no fear, princess!"

"Throw me the sword, knight!" Kai tossed a stick to Gerda. "We will attack from both sides!"

Suddenly, the fanfare sounded, and within seconds, the two could hear a faint stampede of footsteps running down the hallway. Kai nonchalantly jogged over to the door, following all the other guests. In truth, he was so excited, he could hardly wait.

"Come on, Gerda!"

"Wait, Kai, we'll go in a minute. Don't you want to finish?"

"All right." He turned away from the door and dragged his feet over to the couch.

"Hiiiiiyaaah! The princess blasts the dragon into smithereens!"

"Good job, princess!"

"Thank you for coming for me, knight!"

The dragon fallen and the princess saved, Kai wrapped a red scarf around his neck, and Gerda tied her white pinafore over her red dress. Next, she tightened the white bows in her two braids. They both ran down to the courtyard, but were dismayed to see that the party was already well under way. Instead of the usual klezmer band, however, there seemed to be a strange woman, dressed all in white.

The woman looked young. Gerda guessed that she was maybe in her early thirties. Even Kai, not always the most observant, immediately noticed that she stood out from the crowd. She had dark skin that stood out against her white gown, beautiful raven hair, and deep, cold, brown eyes. Suddenly, Gerda realized that snowflakes, that had not been there just minutes ago, were hastily floating over and whirling around the mystery guest, as if blown over by a great gust of wind. It was as if Grandpa Frost himself was carrying them through the air with his great big puffs. Gerda also noticed that the air had become significantly colder. She thought nothing of it until it really could not be dismissed. Gerda thought that she heard the snowflakes singing. Gerda looked to her right at Kai and saw a look of fearful admiration on his face.

"Kai, what are those?" she whispered.

"They are beautiful. But I feel . . . almost scared of their beauty."

The others glanced around, sharing long puzzled looks with their friends. The snowflakes were like a slightly dismal, haunted orchestra. Then, with a huge gust of cold air, the woman began to dance—or rather float—around and around, barely skirting the edge of the crowd. Whenever she got too close to Gerda's liking, Gerda quickly shied away, but not Kai. Gerda tried to grasp Kai's gaze, but he seemed mesmerized by the unordinary presence.

"Will anyone dance with me?" the woman's voice echoed. "Anyone who does will get a kiss—from me."

As if pulled by a string, Kai calmly walked over to the woman and took her hand.

"No! Kai!"

"There's a good, brave boy."

As they waltzed in circles, Gerda had a terrified look on her face. *What is Kai doing? Why won't he look at me?!*

She had an urge to run over to Kai and yank him out of the woman's arms. The woman was tall, but although Kai was just a few weeks older than Gerda, he was almost the woman's height. Then, just as quickly as it had begun, the music stopped and the raging wind assumed the role of accompaniment.

The woman kissed the top of Kai's head, and instantly, Kai's eyes glazed over and he stood frozen, as if in a trance.

"I am the Snow Queen," the mysterious woman majestically announced, "and he," she said, pointing to Kai, "is going with me. I could use some company so high up in the mountains." She wrapped her snow-white cape around herself with a flourish and with Kai still on her arm, she disappeared in a puff of gray smoke.

Gerda's First Encounter

With the Snow Queen gone, Gerda's small shoulders were quaking, and she was gasping for air, almost as if she had been submerged in ice cold water for much too long.

"KAI, NO! COME BACK, COME BACK!" Gerda cried as her body tremored and shook from the still-fresh shock. The scene was replaying over and over in her head. She didn't hear the sobs of Kai's mother or her own screaming her name.

Her mother swept her up into her arms and whispered in Gerda's ear, "It's okay, we'll find him, it's going to be all right," but Gerda could hear the quaver in her voice. Gerda's thoughts seemed to be just as muddled as the fog that was beginning to settle just below the horizon.

What were the chances of finding a boy cast into an unknown corner of this world by a white, stormy, and villainous stranger? The kind that can brew a storm inside you with just a single glare. That glare can destroy any mortal and turn their insides to ice, but with a kiss, their very heart will be frozen forever.

Facing the woods, Gerda unleashed all her sorrow in a burst of energy and ran and ran and ran. Her hair whipping in all directions with not so much as a knapsack on her shoulders to weigh her down, Gerda stumbled. With a start, she woke from her daze and was almost suffocated by the realization of what she had just done. She was in the heart of the forest, a dangerous place, with no food, water, or companion. The events of that evening jolted right back to her, and exhausted, Gerda fell into a tormented sleep.

"Kakraw, Kakraw! Birds of the forest, wake up! And I mean right now! How can I fail to demand attention with my glamorous presence? This is outrageous, the amount of disrespect I am receiving! Humph!"

Through Gerda's blurred vision, she saw a very well groomed crow mumbling to himself and screeching at others.

What on Earth!? Is he talking? Of all the possible things she could have thought after yesterday's ordeal, this crow seemed

to dominate her mind. Gerda looked up at the crow with a sort of inquisitive look to ask whether the bird could repeat itself, just to make sure she heard right.

"Are you . . . talking?"

"Why, of course I am!" The crow protested with a hurt look on his face and scrunched up his eyebrows.

She noticed he was constantly licking his wings and smoothing out his black feathers. His large eyes seemed to protrude from his head, and he wore a vest in a stunning shade of deep blue. The crow's little dialogue and his appearance left Gerda bewildered and utterly confused. Whoever heard of a well-dressed and groomed crow that was quite sufficiently verbose? She looked around to ask someone else if they could hear the crow talking, but there was no one around, except an ant, but Gerda did not want to risk her sanity by conversing with an insect.

The crow cleared its throat. "Pardon me for the impertinent behavior of these, um, birds." Gerda looked up and squeaked in surprise. Lining four branches right above her head were about ten pigeons. "Let me properly introduce myself. I am Sir Krakowsky Petrev Crow. And you are?"

Still gaping, she replied, "Umm . . . Gerda?"

"All right then, Gerda. Firstly, close your mouth. Capisce? Good! Now, move a little to the left; I look best from my right side. Okay, wake the birds? Check. Waste time on little girls? Check. Next, I need to finish constructing my bath. Ta ta!"

"Wait, wait! Stop! Come back, I need your help."

"Fine," Krakowsky sighed. "You have two minutes to give me a reason why I should care."

With Krakowsky's consent, Gerda recounted all of the events of the past day and struggled to keep the tears that were welling in her eyes at bay. She told him about her brotherhood with Kai, the party at New Year's, the icy stranger, Kai's disappearance, running away to find him; everything gushed out.

"That was so moving, my dear child," choked Krakowsky, wiping away his tears and pulling out his handkerchief. He submerged his face in it and emitted a great honk. "And so tragic. I know who that villain is; she wiped out all of the other crows. Only I and my wife remain with these moronic pigeons."

Gerda glanced up at the pigeons and decided that they could not understand anything Krakowsky was saying.

"Long ago, she was called Elizabeth, and was so innocent, kind, and gentle. I used to be her footman. But then she got rid of me, and began her reign of the north. She began with lightly frosting all of the crops around her; she rather enjoyed a season of famine. Still, she was not satisfied. No one knows what made her evil and poisonous towards everything living. Wherever she wanted to settle, she would freeze everything around her and construct an enormous ice castle. She has also frozen people before. Her kiss makes a person evil and gives him a heart of ice, just like hers."

Gerda's eyes widened.

"I think that is what happened to Kai. I'm so sorry, Gerda." Krakowsky hung his head.

"About what, my dear Kraka?" came a shrill, teasing voice from somewhere in the trees.

"That's my Lily."

With a questioning look from Gerda, he continued. "She's

my wife."

"I see . . ." Gerda replied.

"Oh my Krakowsky, how I've missed you! And who is this lovely little girl you've got? Is she an addition to our little colony of ten?" A slightly smaller but equally black crow emerged from the branches, wearing a thin periwinkle ribbon around her neck.

"No, my dear. She has lost her friend Kai, who was taken by the Snow Queen."

"Oh my goodness, I'm so sorry. I know how you feel. Our entire crow population was taken, but I know who can help us. You see, Gerda, I work for Her Majesty Rachelle, and she used to be very well acquainted with Elizabeth before she iced over. Her Majesty may know where the Snow Queen resides."

"Thank you so much for your help, Lily! You too, Krakowsky." Gerda was suddenly overcome by a wave of emotion, and hugged the crow couple so tightly that Krakowsky gasped for her to let them go.

Collecting themselves, Gerda, Krakowsky, and Lily set off to Her Majesty's castle.

Meeting Her Majesty

On top of the high mountain, visible from any point in Vysoky Kingdom, loomed an enormous, thin castle. There were but two towers rising up from the west and east points of it and its once-deep elegant lavender color had faded into a worn-down and dreadful-looking shade of beige-gray. The desperate, hopeless exterior of the castle perfectly matched Princess Rachelle. Restless and trapped, on many occasions, her many maids, Lily included, could see her pacing across her chambers and stopping occasionally to give a yearning glance towards the gray sky.

Gerda knocked, sharply inhaled, and pushed open the door. Inside Her Majesty's chambers, every shelf was filled with old, dusty books that looked like they had not been read in a long time. Books occupied everything except Her Majesty's bedside table. On it rested a frame with a painting of two rosy-cheeked girls, maybe fourteen years old, and a couple of snowflake candle holders.

"Your Majesty, I'm Gerda. My closest friend, Kai, was taken by the Snow Queen yesterday. He is my best friend and is like a brother to me. We had so many things we wanted to do together, and now . . . he's gone. I need to track him down. I need to find him!" Gerda blurted out.

"Gerda wishes to ask you about the Snow Queen's whereabouts," Lily clarified. Rachelle instantly turned a shade paler than she already was. "Un-unless, of course, you are not feeling well," Lily stammered apologetically.

"No, no, it's perfectly all right. I pondered that question for many years myself. If you will excuse us," Rachelle waved all of the other maids away. "Years ago, probably when I was five years old, I first left the castle. Just as we passed the gates into the market, a little girl ran right up to me and said, 'Hi! I'm Elizabeth. What's your name?' She grabbed me by the hand and led me deeper into the market. Stunned, I followed. Even though my nanny trailed behind us, I felt like I was unsupervised and free. From then on, I asked my nanny to take me into town every day, and Elizabeth would wait for me by the peddler's cart that sold citrus."

Gerda's thoughts strayed from Her Majesty's story, and instead

thought about her friendship with Kai.

"Later, probably when I was sixteen or so, I was allowed to go into the market without any supervision. On that day, I first heard Elizabeth mention how much she loved ice, which was odd because it never snowed in Vysoky. When I asked her where she had seen ice, she explained that over the summer, she and her family lived in their cabin in the woods for a little while. She had somehow been able to freeze some water for her to suck on during the heat wave. Out of nowhere, a bear in the forest approached her and asked Elizabeth to come to the tallest mountain in Visota, a neighboring region.

"A bear?" asked Gerda.

"Yes. She evaded my questions that day, but I later found out that Elizabeth turned the brown bear into a polar bear, and he became her guard and pet. Since then, many people and animals met the same fate: pets, guards, and accomplices. So, on that cold October morning, I found out that my trip to the market had been made only to say goodbye. Elizabeth disappeared and never came back."

Like Kai, thought Gerda. She started to put the pieces together: the desolate castle, Her Majesty's sad face. *She understands. Elizabeth was taken away from her and she never recovered.*

"The next day . . . "

Rachelle had been interrupted by heaving sobs coming from somewhere under the table; Krakowsky had hidden underneath his wings.

"Oh, don't cry, Krakowsky. That's life, you know. You just have to keep going." Even while comforting Krakowsky, Gerda couldn't help but notice that Rachelle looked rather sad.

"I haven't seen her in years, but I have heard that she continues to live on the mountain Maguchi in the Visota kingdom. My maids will provide you with warm clothing and a warm bath before you go on your way; it is deathly cold up there. Her castle is hidden, but I can assure you that it lies just on the other end of a tunnel made of rock. Please, be safe. You don't know what Elizabeth is capable of."

The Bandits

Her Majesty Rachelle's castle was right in between the plains, where Gerda's little town lay, and the forest. The only way to Maguchi was through the trees. The deep forest was yet another of Krakowsky's fears, and Gerda could hear Lily and Krakowsky bickering, surely for the first twenty minutes. Krakowsky was constantly pulling twigs out of his feathers, and Lily was scolding him for being so fussy.

"We're in a forest, for Her Majesty's sake! There are twigs!"

"Yes, my dear, but that does not mean that we must abandon all forms of hygiene," Krakowsky snapped back.

Exasperated, Gerda spun around, ready to give the pair a piece of her mind when she heard a cry. All too quickly, the bandits were upon them. *Ugghh! Why was I so stupid? I led us right into bandit territory*, thought Gerda.

They were a terrifying bunch with ragged shirts and baggy trousers. The bandit that had overtaken Gerda, seemingly the leader of the group, had a bald head and a scarred face with one small gold earring in his left ear.

Holding a knife up to Gerda's throat, he rasped, "Our commander Alexandra wants to see you now."

Rightly so, he guessed that Krakowsky was unwaveringly loyal to Gerda, and would never leave her. Lily and Krakowsky were equally

devoted to each other and would never leave the other, so the bandit didn't bother tying their wings.

He shoved the trio down onto their knees. Just beneath her nose, Gerda saw a pair of boots that seemed to go all the way to the knee, then a red skirt, then a billowing black blouse, and finally a bandana around a head, exploding with a mass of dark brown curls. The leader had two gold earrings and an emerald pendant around her neck.

"Good work, Antonin," she said as she tossed him a gold coin. He caught it and retreated behind the trees.

Alexandra spun slow, lazy circles around Gerda and Lily. She seemed to have completely forgotten about Krakowsky.

"I rather like your muffs. Oh, and that hat. Fancy. Boys, she probably has more. I can smell quality soap on this one."

The other bandits jumped out from behind the trees and shuffled around in search of more goods. Finding nothing, they sulked back to their leader.

"Fine, hand those over and you can go," she snarled at Gerda, grabbing her arm. Gerda slowly took off her hat and muffs and tossed them to Alexandra. Alexandra let go of Gerda, but Gerda noticed that she kept a tight grip on Lily.

"Let her go," Gerda said in a quavering voice. Alexandra ignored her.

"I know most everything that goes on in this kingdom. I also happen to know that you," Alexandra said, jabbing Lily in the chest, "are a maid to Rachelle. Her family outcast me to these desperate woods. I have to live here with these idiots." She glanced around at her flunkies. "I want you," Alexandra spat, again pointing at Lily, "to tell Rachelle to let me back in. I get the clothes and a ticket back into the kingdom, and you get to continue through these woods. Those are my conditions. Accept them, and your friends can go. If not . . . " Alexandra let that last sentence linger.

Krakowsky sprung protectively to Lily's side. Staring straight ahead, she mulled over Alexandra's ultimatum. "Fine. I will ask. But Her Majesty might not consent to it."

"Ah, but she will." Alexandra's eyes flickered and Gerda was starting to think that maybe Alexandra had some unfinished business with Her Majesty Rachelle. "You must leave now. Antonin, go with the lady crow to the castle."

"Yes, ma'am," he responded from somewhere behind her.

"Now?" Lily gasped.

"No!" cried Krakowsky.

"I guess that girl and your crow will have to journey on their own. Unless, of course, you would like to stay with us," Alexandra suggested, feigning generosity.

All eyes were on Lily. Alexandra's eyes were burning, daring Lily to challenge her. Gerda's eyes stared imploringly at Lily, knowing she would never reach Kai unless the bandits let them through. Antonin looked on the scene with frustrated eyes, not wanting to make the long trek to the castle. Krakowsky's eyes were open wide and he shook his head to Lily, trying to make her refuse the ultimatum. Lily sadly nodded her head, sighed, hugged Krakowsky tightly, whispered something in Gerda's ear, and took off, with Antonin yelling as he struggled to keep up.

"You may go, and I will keep these as tokens," Alexandra said as she waggled the muffs in front of Gerda's face. Boys, leave them

be. They can go."

As Gerda and Krakowsky continued through the forest, Gerda couldn't help but wonder what other encounters lay ahead of them. They hadn't even reached the mountains yet. Who knew what dangers awaited there? Gerda refused to accept or even think about the horrible things that may have happened to Kai in the past two days. She refused to think about what she would do if Kai wasn't at the Snow Queen's castle. Right now, it was her only plan and her only hope to reach Kai in time, before his heart froze completely. Throughout the journey, she recognized the aching in her heart and the whirling thoughts as she was falling asleep to be deep worry and love for Kai, and she missed him terribly. Often, Krakowsky suggested turning back, but with Kai's face in mind, Gerda was driven onward. She knew it was too late to turn back, and too early to give up.

To be continued . . .

Viewpoint

Kristi Wright worked with Liana Zhu to finesse which character's perspective all of the important information comes from in Liana's story, "Bling and the S.G."

Dear Reader,

In "Bling and the S.G.," Liana Zhu's clever use of pen pal letters to relay information about her characters results in an entertaining and unique story about two unlikely friends.

For Liana's revision, we focused on viewpoint (also known as point of view). Viewpoint refers to the perspective a story is being told from. Which character is having all the thoughts and emotional reactions in the story? Typically, it should be the character the readers will most relate to. In short stories, writers tend to use a single viewpoint, focusing on one character's thoughts and emotions. In novels, writers often stick to single viewpoint, but they also may choose to use multiple viewpoints, allowing more than one character to help tell the story.

In Liana's tale, the primary viewpoint character is Hanna, and Liana does a fabulous job of showing us her thoughts and reactions, making her both relatable and appealing. We become intimately acquainted with Hanna as we see her react to who her new pen pal is and then to the actual pen pal letters. On the other hand, we only see Riley's thoughts if he chooses to reveal them within his pen pal letters.

In Liana's original draft, there were a few moments when we stepped out of Hanna's viewpoint and into someone else's. This isn't necessarily a bad thing to do. Strategic use of multiple viewpoints can be a wonderful way to help readers fall in love with more than one character. But switches in viewpoint can be a little jolting and sometimes even confusing, especially in a shorter work.

Since "Bling and the S.G." was already mostly in one viewpoint, it felt well suited to being transformed into a single viewpoint story. Together, Liana and I identified spots where viewpoint shifted away from Hanna, and then Liana rewrote those sections to keep them consistently in Hanna's point of view.

The next time you write or revise a story, check who is having the thoughts in it. Is it just one character or are multiple characters revealing their thoughts and emotions? If you have multiple viewpoints in your work, ask yourself whether it's critical to the story to switch viewpoints, or is it something you did without thinking about it? Figure out who your main character is and then study each of the other viewpoint characters to determine how important it is for their perspective be communicated. Can a character's thoughts show up in dialogue instead? Or, as with Liana's story, in a letter?

Play with viewpoint. Make conscious decisions about who is telling the story. Have fun experimenting with single viewpoint and multiple viewpoint!

Happy writing,
Kristi Wright

Kristi Wright is the Assistant Regional Advisor for the San Francisco/South region of the Society of Children's Books Writers and Illustrators. She offers writing workshops at elementary schools with a focus on viewpoint and sensory detail. She is also the assistant editor for a blog that analyzes middle grade novels as mentor text for writers: *www.mglunchbreak.com*. Her indie-published futuristic middle grade adventure series, The Basker Twins in the 31st Century, raises funds and awareness for a rare, childhood-onset disease, Friedreich's ataxia. She lives in Northern California with her husband and three furry friends—a lovable but wacky dog and two cats, one mostly sweet and the other mostly dangerous. Find her at www. *kristiwrightauthor.com* and on Twitter @KristiWrite.

Liana Zhu

Liana is nine years old, and heading into fourth grade at Living Wisdom School. She lives in Palo Alto, California, with her parents, Nan and Minyao; her younger sister, Madelyn; and her betta fish, Rainbow. In her free time, she loves to make jewelry, sketch, and doodle. She also enjoys playing piano. If she could visit anywhere, she'd visit a tropical island because she could snorkel there. Her favorite colors are lavender and aqua blue. Her favorite foods are seaweed and sushi.

Kristi Wright: What inspired you to write "Bling and the S.G."?
Liana Zhu: I met a new friend while on a cruise, but she lived in New York, so we became pen pals. I thought a pen pal story would be a good idea. Also, I love jewelry making, so I thought one character could be like me.

Q: What inspired you to use the letters as your narrative device?
A: It's unique and different, and since it was about two pen pals, I thought they would mostly talk to each other that way.

Q: Have you ever had a pen pal? What was the experience like?
A: I still have a pen pal I spoke about. She lives in New York. I love getting her letters, and sending mine back. Once, she even sent a slide show of her favorite pictures.

Q: What was your favorite part of "Bling and the S.G."?
A: My favorite part is how the problem gets resolved, because there's always a way to fix problems if you try. When Bling finds out that Riley is in coding class too, she feels relieved.

Q: How did you feel about focusing on viewpoint for your revision?

A: I thought it was a good suggestion to focus on. Otherwise, the story wouldn't make sense in those parts.

Q: Do you like how your story changed through the revision process?

A: It only changed a bit, and it feels much better. When I was in the middle of writing it, I didn't notice all the changed viewpoints.

Q: What advice would you give other writers about revision?

A: Revision helps you notice your deeper story. Every writer needs feedback, and every writer needs revision—a lot of it!

Q: How long have you been writing?

A: I've been writing since first grade. I didn't like writing in first and second grade, because I had writer's block. I started to like writing in third grade when I found my "inner writer."

Q: Are you writing anything now?

A: Yes! I'm writing a lot of things, including a Chinese New Year play, and a story about annoying people!

Q: What are some of your favorite books?

A: I like the Mrs. Piggle-Wiggle series because it is so imaginative. Also, I like *The Candymakers* by Wendy Mass. The setting has a whole new world full of mouth-watering candies!

Q: What other things do you like to do? Do you like to do any of the things your characters like to do?

A: Yes, I like jewelry making like Bling, and some sports like soccer and tae kwon do. I also do coding, but I'm not very good at it yet. I'm learning to type now so I can write stories faster.

Bling and the S.G.

by

Liana Zhu

anna woke up this morning feeling super excited.

"Today is the pen pal surprise day!" she shouted out loud, thinking *I'm sure that I'm going to get to be pen pals with my friend Kate Samson at Churchill Elementary. She told me that she's getting pen pals in her class, too.* She threw on her clothes, finished breakfast, and yelled goodbye to her mother as she grabbed her backpack and raced off to school.

Miss Abby was announcing, "Today you'll get your pen pals! I know you're going to love writing to them!" Kids were whispering to each other. "Now settle down, class, and you'll learn your partner names."

"Who am *I* getting?" interrupted Timmy Webber.

"Timmy, this is the last time I will remind you to not interrupt!"

Hanna could tell he was blushing and felt embarrassed.

"Now, I'm writing the names of your pen pals on the board. All these students are at Churchill Elementary, in fourth grade."

Hanna held her breath, and nobody made a sound.

Miss Abby began to write out a list. It began with, "Tim gets Carlos Ruiz . . . " At the fourteenth pair, her name finally appeared on the board.

And there it was. "Hanna gets Riley Thompson."

Hanna felt hollow inside. *NOT* what she was expecting! But wait! *Isn't Riley in Kate's class? Maybe Riley probably hangs out with Kate. I hope she likes jewelry making like me.*

Then, Miss Abby announced, "Here are the letters of introduction from your pen pals," as she handed out their first letters.

Hanna unfolded a crumpled letter. To her surprise, a school photo of Riley was taped at the top: a tall freckled boy with spiky brown hair. A boy! *NOT A GIRL!* Hanna was in shock.

Feb. 3

Dear Hanna,

I am in 4th grade at Churchill. You have 14 girls in your class, but we have only 13, so my teacher made me have a girl pen pal. I like basketball and soccer. Do you like sports?

Your New Pen Pal,
Riley Thompson

Hanna stuffed the letter in her backpack, and laid her head on the desk, holding back tears of disappointment.

"This is not going to be a good pen pal project," she grumbled.

"Every Monday, you will receive a new pen pal letter. Every

Monday night, your homework is to write back to your pen pal," instructed Miss Abby. "Have fun! Be sure to sign your name! Put it in the homework basket tomorrow morning."

The next morning, Hanna stomped into class and shoved an incomplete letter into the homework basket. It read,

Feb. 4

Dear Riley,
You're a boy, I'm a girl. I don't like any sports, not even gymnastics. I like jewelry making. Have a nice day.

Your Pen Pal,
Hanna Quinley

At the school lunch table, everybody was excitedly sharing news of their pen pals, all the things they had in common. Hanna kept silent, chewing her tuna sandwich. She was thinking, *This is going to be a horrible month of writing to a boy pen pal. After all, I don't like writing anyway.* The following Monday, she got Riley's next letter.

Feb. 10

Dear Hanna,
I am on the Rockets Team. I made 5 baskets this week! One was a miracle-long-distance shot! Did you see the Warriors vs. the Lakers on T.V. on Saturday? They were amazing, huh?!

I hope I get to play professional someday. You sound like a pretty nice person and I like writing to you.

Riley

This letter sounded odd.

"Maybe Riley read my letter wrong." Hanna stuffed it into her desk and groaned, "He doesn't sound as disappointed as I am."

Miss Abby told the class, "In your friendly letter, be sure to include a nice comment about their news, a question, and explain your news in your next response."

The next evening, Hanna wrote back.

Feb. 11

Dear Riley,

Sounds like you had fun in your game. I do not watch basketball. I watch the BBC jewelry making show. I just learned how to make Rainbow Loom bracelets. Have you ever seen Taylor Swift wearing her one carat diamond ring when she sings on T.V.? Don't you think jewelry makes people around the world more beautiful? Have you ever seen photos of how beautiful Queen Elizabeth looks in her emerald necklace? One day I plan to have a jewelry shop, and I'll design my own jewelry. Everybody calls me Bling because I love to wear jewelry. I once saw that some basketball players wear gold earrings, gold chains, and crosses.

Do you wear any jewelry?

Your pen pal,
Hanna

At lunchtime, everybody still talked about their pen pals like they just got them that day. She silently picked at her lunch, too frustrated to eat.

"This can't go on! He's no fun at all. What's the point of writing?" She zipped her lunch bag. The next Monday, she got Riley's reply.

Feb. 17

Dear Hanna,
My basketball team won last week, and guess what?! We're going to the Junior Championship playoffs! We have cool team uniforms, red and black colors. I don't have any jewelry. I made a slam dunk yesterday. Wish me luck at the finals.

Your pen pal,
Riley

On Monday afternoon, Hanna stayed late and plopped herself on Miss Abby's "I need help" chair and sighed, "I don't like my pen pal, not one bit. Can't I have a different one?"

"Hmm?" replied Miss Abby, looking up from her pile of worksheets she was correcting. "Have you tried to talk with your

pen pal?"

"We don't have *anything* in common," Hanna whined.

She replied, "There will always be *something* in common. Ask him what his hobby is, what his favorite food is, does he have siblings, or pets, and what does he like to read. We can't change pen pals. That would be rude." Hanna fumed on the walk home, but reluctantly wrote him again.

Feb. 18

Dear Riley,

My favorite soccer team is "The Nobodies." Sorry, but I don't like soccer or basketball, either. Or baseball, or hockey, or football. I HATE sports! So I'm supposed to ask you. What is your favorite food? What's your hobby? Do you have a sibling? How old? Do you have a pet? What do you like to read?

Your pen pal,
Hanna

"Blah . . . blah . . . blah!" She was still moody as she turned in her homework letter to Ms. Abby. His answer came back the following Monday.

Feb. 24

Dear Hanna,

I have a dog I named Stephen Curry. I like Round Table cheese pizza. My basketball team goes there after the games. I have a little brother, Andrew, but I call him Score, because I'm teaching him free throws. I read sports biographies about famous players like Kobe Bryant on the Lakers. I want to be an S.G. like him—that means "shooting guard." Do you have any brothers or sisters that play basketball? Have you ever made sports wristbands for soaking up sweat? I could hecka use one of those! I can't write much today, because I have to get to my new coding class.

Your pen pal,
Riley

"*Really*?!" Hanna's jaw dropped as she read the last sentence. "He's *really* going to a coding class? I'm in a coding class, too! I wonder what level he's on." Finally, they had found something in common! She wrote back immediately.

Feb. 25

Dear Riley,
Do you really have a coding class? So do I! I'm using Tynker! Are you using Tynker? If so, what level are you on? Are you making a project?"

Sincerely,
Hanna

March 4

Dear Hanna,

I'm also using Tynker, but I'm stuck on Level 10, and it's getting very tedious. I keep copying the same pattern over and over again. About 30 times! It says, go another 40 times! No way! Can you help me?

Your Pen Pal,
Riley

March 5

Hi Riley,

I have finished coding Tynker level 10. You should use the REPEAT command. Look for it in the list of commands at the bottom of the "popular usage" list. Let me know if that helps.

Hanna

She couldn't believe it. She *wanted* to read Riley's letter and write back to him!

March 12

Dear Hanna

*Thanks! I finally passed level 10 in Tynker. I'm working in Coding Genius now. Have you tried it? I'm building a basketball game. It's going to be **the Blingers vs. the Warriors**. I'm putting you on the Blingers team, and*

I'm on the Warriors. What do you want for the Blingers team colors?

PS. My basketball team's going to the Junior Championship Finals!

Wish me luck,
Riley

March 19

Dear Riley,
I haven't tried Coding Genius. Make the Blingers wear gold and purple, please. Could you show me your coded basketball game on an iPad when I visit you at Churchill for the Pen Pal Meet-up next week? Aren't your basketball team's colors black and red? I have enclosed a good-luck-friendship band I made for you. Good luck on your championship!

Your Pen Pal/coding friend,
Bling

March 26

Dear Hanna,
Thank you for the friendship bracelet. I love how you found the basketball charm and added it on to the friendship bracelet to make it fancier. It really helped me score the last hoop for my team to win

the championships! If someone congratulates me, I'll give half of the credit to you. I just finished the coded basketball game, and can't wait to show it to you.

See you at the pen pal meetups!
S.G.

On the following Sunday, Hanna was impatiently waiting for lunchtime so her mother could drive her to Churchill Elementary. She made three bracelets while waiting. Finally, the clock alarm rung at twelve o'clock, and Mom woke up from her nap.

"Let's go now, Mom!" Hanna excitedly shouted, slipping on her sequined jogging shoes. When they reached Churchill, a crowd of students in cars were arriving in the parking lot. As she climbed out of her car, she noticed a tall boy with spiky brown hair standing by the entrance gate.

"Hey Riley, is that you?" she shouted over the loud idling of car engines.

He nodded and smiled, and she noticed he was carrying an iPad under his arm.

"Thanks for your good luck bracelet, Bling! It helped me win the championship! Oh, and I brought the coding game to show you," he exclaimed.

Bling smiled as they headed towards his classroom.

Tone and Word Choice

Sonja Solter guided Alexa Friesel on choosing exactly the right words to convey the tone in her poem, "Growing Up."

Dear Reader,

The tone of a poem, which is the author's feelings and attitude about the subject of the poem, might seem difficult to revise because it can feel hard to pin down. Many aspects of the poem work together to create tone, and it also often feels like tone just flows out of us naturally as we write. In the case of "Growing Up," Alexa was already communicating the tone of her poem quite well. I had a strong sense of her ambivalence towards the growing-up process and her feeling of being stuck in between the past and the future.

Alexa and I decided that working with her choice of words could help her get across her tone even more clearly. Alexa's word choices were often already quite specific to her tone. For example, when she said, "I long to run freely across to the future," the choice of "freely" was the perfect complement for her to "long" for, while feeling "stuck."

Sometimes a word or phrase is already a pretty good fit for the tone, but playing around with other possibilities can uncover an even better choice. With this in mind, Alexa decided to go through her poem word by word several times, trying out various word choices. An example of a change she made that she felt better fit her tone was: "I don't want to see that kind of light," which she changed to "I'm scared to see that kind of light." "Scared" gives the reader a more specific feel for how the stuckness between the past and the future feels for the author.

We often just pick what comes to us naturally as we write, and these are often good choices. However, I encourage you to give revision a try, even for parts of your writing that seem pretty good already. There may be an even better fit out there!

Remember, it is not always cut-and-dried; sometimes a particular choice is playing another role, and you may decide to leave it as-is. That is absolutely your right as the author. Just make sure you allow yourself to play around because that "playing," even if you think you will leave a part the same, is really the skill of revision itself. So, every time you do it, you will become a better reviser in the future.

Here's to lots of possibilities and choices!

Sonja Solter

Sonja Solter lives in Colorado with her husband, two children, and very cuddly doodle-mix puppy. She enjoys reading and traveling to places both near and far. Her favorite place to be outdoors is in a dense forest. She is currently revising her middle-grade novel-in-verse and brainstorming a picture book biography.

Alexa Friesel

Alexa is in seventh grade at Castilleja. She is thirteen years old. She enjoys horseback riding and debate. She'd like to be a lawyer or work in marketing someday. In addition to poetry, she likes to write realistic fiction and dystopia.

Sonja Solter: How did the revision process go for you? What was the hardest part of revising?

Alexa Friesel: In the revision process, I changed a couple of words to make it feel more how I wanted it to feel—less generic, and more how I would feel. Once I found the spot to revise, it was easy, but finding the spots was difficult. I was able to do it by reading it over a lot and by trying to imagine it. If I had trouble imagining it, then I knew something wasn't right.

Q: What advice do you have for other Inklings who don't like revision very much?

A: Just think about making your piece the best it can be, read it over a lot, and eventually you will find something to revise.

Q: When did you start writing? Are you working on anything right now?

A: I started writing in kindergarten when we were writing picture books for class. I remember loving it when I first tried it. I'm happy doing any kind of writing. I enjoy writing because I love to create things and be able to make a world. I also like to be able to express myself through a story or poem. I'm writing a realistic fiction novel right now that I've been working on.

Q: Who do you enjoy sharing your writing with?

A: I usually don't share my writing, but sometimes I'll share it with my friends or teachers.

Q: Do you ever feel blocked? If so, what do you do?

A: I get writer's block all the time. Sometimes when I get writer's block, I'll look at the internet or photos for inspiration. Sometimes my English teacher gives me a writing prompt, which helps. But sometimes I'll just look around and see where it takes me.

Growing Up

by

Alexa Friesel

A bridge between two worlds
I long to run freely across to the future
See this new world for myself
The ropes of memory hold me back

I long to run freely across to the future
The stars there seem so bright
But the brightness finds a way to burn
I'm scared to see that kind of light

The stars there seem so bright
Time will come and pass
Across is where my days should last
But fear will hold me back

Time will come and pass
Footsteps across the bridge at night
Birds sound at light
It always is the same

Footsteps across the bridge at night
This time they are my own
They push me across, then back again
To where I was once before

This time they are my own
Ideas to cross and to stay
But I do as I am told
And it repeats once again

Ideas to cross and to stay
I am stuck in the middle
Stuck in the middle of what to do
I am fully immersed in this all

I am stuck in the middle
Forever trapped on this bridge
Running back and forth
Until I am where I belong

Heart of the Story

Jamieson Haverkampf showed Ksenia Baatz how to examine her character's motivations to uncover the main theme in her story, "Colored."

Dear Reader,

Short stories are short. When you write one, each word or sentence must relate back to the heart of the story (or "theme") you want to express to readers. One way to enhance the message at the heart of a story is to amplify the main character's motivations—which is what Ksenia decided to do with her main character, Chloe, in the short story, "Colored."

Ksenia and I agreed on the heart of her story that we would enhance: *In challenging situations, we each have the power to make new choices that support things that matter deeply to our hearts.* There are three important elements writers can use to reveal a character's deeper motivations: the goal (what specifically does Chloe want?); the stakes (what happens if Chloe doesn't get what she wants?); and the obstacles (what challenges must Chloe face as she attempts to achieve her goal?). Together, we reviewed opportunities where Ksenia could strengthen Chloe's emotions and reactions to enhance the heart of the story.

At the end of our first call, Ksenia asked me a (fantastic) question before tackling her revision: *What are some techniques to show more of Chloe's emotions such as panic, fear, or anger related to her goal, stakes, or obstacles?*

The first way humans experience emotion is through a physically felt signal coming from our bodies. Writers use these physical reactions to reveal our characters' emotions. For example, when we're afraid, we might feel the small hairs standing up on the back of our necks or our hands might sweat and feel clammy. Or when we're nervous, our stomachs might feel like they're knotted up like a pretzel. That said, here's the best way to show a character's emotion: First, close your eyes and remember the physical signals your body sends that alert you to know you're experiencing a new emotion such as anger. Then, write your character experiencing those same physical signals you receive when you first realize you are angry.

By choosing powerful sensory images such as a blanket, a tilted scale weighted down to one side, and magical colored pencils, Ksenia allowed readers to relate through the senses in their bodies to the emotions Chloe experiences—while, at the same time, emphasizing the heart of the story. When writers use sensory objects for the main character to experience one way at the beginning and show how those same objects change by the end of the story, it reveals a character's emotional shift and how that character has changed since the story's beginning.

The more you reveal emotion through a felt sense experienced in a character's body, the more readers will relate to and root for your character to succeed. In these next pages, you'll see how Ksenia convinced me to care about and root for Chloe and soon you'll be rooting for Chloe too. And remember: short stories may be short, but they can still make our hearts swell and grow a little taller.

Happy writing,
Jamieson Haverkampf

With seven years of experience working with middle and high school teens at the private Atlanta Girls School and her MFA in Writing for Young Adults from Hamline University, Jamieson Haverkampf deeply values and relates to teens and their creative writing. She loves stories packed with magic, humor, rebels, or sleuths and enjoys writing about identity and underdogs. Jamieson also holds degrees in Human Development (Vanderbilt) and in Communication Arts and Design/Illustration (VCU) and her publications include "The Saw Girl," a personal essay about life-changing dreams in the anthology *Dreams That Change Our Lives*, and an award-winning adult resource guidebook, *Mom Minus Dad*. Currently, Jamieson is finishing her first middle grade fantasy novel, exploring her nighttime dreams in her weekly dream group, and planning a big trip to Scotland and Ireland to learn more about her Celtic/British Isles ancestry and hopefully dig up a few new stories!

Ksenia Baatz

Sixth-grader Ksenia dwells in Illinois with her parents, grandma, pilose St. Bernard, and cantankerous cat. She loves to write poetry and envisage stories while she is practicing tennis, and overall savors the outdoors, no matter the season. She also adores drawing and investigating the realms of science while creating new stories from her discoveries.

Jamieson Haverkampf: During revision, what changed for you as you considered how Chloe's motivation affected the heart of the story?

Ksenia Baatz: When I first wrote this story, I expected it to have a much smaller audience. But after it was one of the winning stories in the Inklings Book Contest and I read my Inklings mentor's editorial letter, I looked deeper at Chloe's emotions. While revising, I noticed I was almost chatting with a character while I wrote about them and it felt like I was just reporting what the character said to me. After I finished the first revision, I thought more about interviewing my characters for the stories I plan to write in the future.

Q: How did you come up with the idea for this story?

A: I interviewed a second-grade girl at my school and a lot of things she said didn't make any sense to me. She talked about tango dancing, a cat, a dragon, and leaves all in the same sentence. But one thing I did understand was that she loved creativity. And it made **me** wonder what life would be like without creativity. I got the idea that the best symbolic way to show life without creativity was to create a world of without color.

Q: What do you love most about writing a story?
A: I love how I can create a character's own reality and always tweak it to the way I want it to be. I get annoyed when I read stories sometimes and I can't tweak the character's reality. But when I write my own stories, I'm always in control and can tweak the reality of the story and make it my own.

Q: What are your favorite books?
A: *The Outsiders* by S.E. Hinton. Some people say that "Colored" is similar to *The Giver*—I like that story a lot, too. Another one of my favorites is *Конёк Горбунок* (*The Humped Horse*), a Russian story my grandma used to read to me as a young girl.

Q: Where do you like to write?
A: I don't have a specific place really, but I do need quiet to write so I can tune into my own mind. It's hard for me to write when there are people running around where I'm sitting or if cats are biting my toes.

Q: Are you working on a new story?
A: Yes. My title for it now is "My Name is Lucky the Slave." It's about a girl who lives in Africa who is taken to America as a slave in the 1600s. I compare and contrast her home and life in Africa to her new home and life in America.

Q: What advice do you have for other Inklings who don't like to revise very much?
A: I'd suggest they take the part of their story they like the best, dissect it, and see what they could improve.

Colored

by

Ksenia Baatz

s I waited outside school, all I could think of was why this world
was gray. No variations, no differences, just gray. The sky was a
stubborn murky ash with the milky clouds oozing sluggishly around
the stark white sun. The wind murmured, caught in the tall, stately
trees. I sighed, a low, long sound that rolled across my lips and
fluttered my uncontrollable hair.

I wished the book, *A Wrinkle in Time*, was not banned. It was
my absolute favorite. The ideas of piercing space, traveling through
time, and exploring wild worlds intrigued me to no end. In old texts, I
had found where my ancient ancestors wrote about the word "color."
They described color as a dynamic blanket that enveloped the world
and made people look unique, new and elegant. Yet, when I looked
at the world, I saw the ash leaves, and the silver sheen that glistened
on all of our lead-colored skin. Was this color? Where was this blanket
that was meant to float onto all our bodies and kiss us with the elixir
of color?

Dr. Grey, our principal, insisted that books were a waste of time, mere entertainment. Instead of books, he encouraged math, science, and history, which he labeled as practical studies. I loved math, but it was only rules—there was no flexibility. When I looked at the world, I saw life as an ever-changing scale. One side was glowing, ubiquitous, and creative. The other was strict, cubed, and sorted into divine symmetry. Now the balance had been tilted; the once-polished stacks of meticulous rules were overwhelming and now seemed like prison bars that programmed my every move.

I was confused by all the changes that had been attacking my daily life and decided to sit down. Instead of the swish from the ash-colored grass, a loud crinkle assaulted my ears. I rocketed up and saw that a mysterious coal-colored package had materialized. On it my name, Chloe, was written in a chalky, swirling script. My parents said that my name meant a young, green plant shoot. I always pondered what the word "green" meant. Maybe it was a mystical creature or a waiting-to-be-discovered planet! Most likely, it was some long-forgotten word.

As I began to unwrap my mysterious present, I heard the school bell ring. I rushed into my seat in the front right corner and noticed that Mrs. Periwinkle's posters were taken down. Mrs. Periwinkle was my beloved teacher who, in secret, taught us creativity. She never said that we were doing something illegal by listening to her, but we all secretly knew that we were breaking the rules. Mrs. Periwinkle introduced poetry and creative writing in short steps. First came the haikus, then longer poems, like sonnets. She taught us about Shakespeare and Madeleine L'Engle, the author of *A Wrinkle in Time*. Soon, she was teaching us creative storytelling, and every morning, we would sit by the glowing fireplace in her classroom and tell our stories one at a time. It was at this time I did not only feel a fuzzy warmth on my skin but also inside.

As I clambered inside my crudely carved desk, my hands were already itching to unwrap my enigmatic present. The teachers never liked to waste time waiting for late students to arrive to school. They were so naïve that they gave us fifteen minutes after the bell rang to settle down and relax. As I unwrapped my present, I allowed the drone of my classmates to fall back as I settled my eyes on a magical treasure. They were a pack of pencils, but instead of being every shade of gray imaginable, they were completely something strange and new I'd never seen before.

Each pencil was labeled a different name. The one labeled "purple" was dark and velvety. Another called "orange" reminded me of my cat. I named him Cinnamon after my favorite food, cinnamon rolls. Cinnamon was friendly and gentle one moment, and fierce, protective, and noble the next, just like the energy of the pencil named orange. Finally, I zeroed down on a single pencil labeled "green." It was bright yet calm, playful, yet it could be used as a somber color. I immediately knew it was for me.

In the very right corner, there was one more pencil. It was a mix of all the pencils, from the one labeled sunny "yellow" to the one labeled deep melancholy "blue." This pencil was called "color all." All the pencils created a spark that made me want to slash the prison bars and free myself of the confines I had lulled myself into. I wanted to screech, to bawl the words out of my mouth and have them leak into everyone's brains to unlock the foolery that gulled us behind the prison bars of rules. Yet the first step was to investigate. My eyes

flickered to the seal of the unopened package as my fingers clawed it off.

Just as I was about to reach for the pencils and try them on paper, I heard the door creak open and slam shut. I looked up, and instead of Mrs. Periwinkle's grandmotherly presence, Dr. Grey's angular shape slunk into the room. While Mrs. Periwinkle smelled of fresh baked pies and cozy autumn evenings, Dr. Grey reminded me of lab-coat-shrouded people bustling around the science lab trying to find a positive use for a possibly destructive chemical that they had created. When Dr. Grey slunk in, a hush fell over my class. He smirked and spoke in a quiet yet commanding voice.

"Mrs. Periwinkle has been fired for endangering your precious little selves and polluting your little minds." Here he paused, relishing the shocked looks on our faces. His voice reminded me of nails screeching of a blackboard or my absolute pet peeve, a high-pitched screaming. "Class is dismissed for today," he almost whispered, daring us to not obey.

He stood in the front of the room waiting for us to file out. I was the last person to dash out of that room and noticed how Dr. Grey positively smirked as he waved me along.

As I exited the school, I noticed that my pencils were gone. I had left them all in the classroom, except for my "color-all" pencil. As I dashed back, I froze in the doorway and immediately hid myself behind the half open door. Dr. Grey was holding my pencils in his hand. I saw him grimace and suddenly, the bright, vibrant colors all faded to dull grays. Dr. Grey gave a sickly smile, dropped the pencils, and slithered out of the room.

The events of the morning flashed before my eyes. The dull

clank of the pencils cracking against the floor echoed in my brain. The way Dr. Grey's lips formed the odious words that delivered the news of Mrs. Periwinkle being fired. The way I, for a moment, had the hope that I could reverse the tilt in the scale and steady my awry life. I rushed into my classroom, still shocked by what I had seen. I picked up the slivered pencils and gently cradled them in my hand. Right there and then, I knew what the "color-all" pencil was meant to do. I pressed the nib of the "color all" pencil to the darkest of all the pencils, and it began to change. Its fractured sides immediately reverted to their usual straight selves, the dull black regained a gossamer sheen, and finally, the pencil became its original color's name: enchanting blue.

After returning all the pencils to their usual color, I began to notice that the floor around the colored pencils was not as gray as it used to be. I scribbled on the floor and it became a light, rosy pink. I do not remember how I knew the word pink, but it seemed to have been locked away somewhere in the back of my mind. While the old floor was riddled with bumps and scratches, this new floor was smooth and spotless. I ran across the room, allowing the color-all pencil to scrape against the desks, the walls, the chairs, and even once, when I jumped, I was able to hit the ceiling. After I had given the whole room a dose of my "color-all," I whirled around and observed as the room lost every speck of gray. The desks became something called pastel blues while Mrs. Periwinkle's desk became a color called sugarplums. The fireplace was a luminous color called yellow while the ceiling and the walls became an unfathomable color called emerald. Laughing, I ran across the school, returning it back to its ancient state.

After I had finished every cranny and crevice in the school, I

rushed outside. I loved nature as it was, but to rid it of all its shades of gray was pure delight. Our school bordered a forest and a small burbling brook. The forest had been left alone, and years of neglect had made it overgrown and polluted. The moment my pencil touched the first tree, the colors green and brown spread, jumping from limb to limb and clearing the trash as they went along. Since it was autumn, it looked like the trees were ablaze, each limb covered in trillions of golden fires. After looking at the forest, I rushed to the brook. It was a murky gray, but the moment I dipped the pencil called blue in, it became a clear but vibrant ultramarine. Exhausted, I galloped home, ready for a long day of rest.

The next morning, after gulping down my favorite breakfast, I rushed to school, excited to see my classmates' reactions. I arrived long before anybody else was there and raced into the classroom. Now when I had paused and looked at the room, it looked elfish, playful, and suited for what Mrs. Periwinkle used to teach. I sighed. I really missed my teacher. Suddenly, I heard a muffled cry coming from Dr. Grey's office. Luckily, his door was unlocked, and I raced in. The room was all black and empty, except for a chair in the middle. In that chair, to my surprise, sat Mrs. Periwinkle, tied up. I immediately freed her and slumped down next to her on the floor gasping, in surprise.

"Thank you, Chloe, thank you," Mrs. Periwinkle whispered, out of breath. "I hope . . . " She trailed off into a coughing fit. "I hope you got my package." She looked out the open door at the colorful orange hallway and smiled.

"Wait, it was you? You gave me the pencils!" I half screamed, half whispered, too excited to be discreet.

"Yep, that was me. Now let's go. Dr. Grey will be entering the school soon." She spat his name out with a scowl.

While I walked down the hallway with her, Mrs. Periwinkle began to explain the backstory to the colored pencils.

"Dr. Grey used to be my student. He was a bright student, smart and clever. The only thing that disturbed him was change. He liked to always have rules to step on, guidelines to work with. That is why he hates creativity so much. With creativity, there are no rules; there are no guidelines. It just bothered him. One day, when he was still a budding scientist, he found a formula that eradicated color, banning it. He went around the world trying to convince people that his invention was wonderful, but nobody found it interesting. Instead, they expelled it and labeled it dangerous. Dr. Grey was so livid that he disobeyed the orders and released a dose of his, how should I call it, medicine. I was able to hide these pencils in a quarantine until the medicine had done its work and a smart little girl like you came along."

I listened raptly as I helped Mrs. Periwinkle into her desk chair. When I looked up at her, I noticed that she was not black and white anymore; she looked unique, new, and elegant as if a dynamic blanket had covered her. Was this "color" that my ancestors had written about in the old texts? It must be. Mrs. Periwinkle laughed at my shock and nodded towards the mirror. I too had been wrapped in this wild blanket called color. I had, as were described in the ancient texts, golden shining hair and chestnut brown eyes. I giggled in pleasant surprise. The unbalanced scale seemed to be tilting in the direction I had dreamed of. Just as my smile stretched across my face, the door slammed, and I heard a hiccup. Dr. Grey was standing

in the doorway, crying.

"Why is it so hard for people to see that I just can't survive in color?" He wheezed through tears, as his body slowly filled with color.

He had onyx black hair with streaks of silver running through, pasty skin, and sunken and tired blue eyes.

Dr. Grey hiccupped before ranting on. "It's just unpredictable, so different, that it scares me," Dr. Grey said. His towering figure shook with heaving sobs.

I looked at his grief-stricken figure, the way his body trembled like an autumn leaf in a gust of winter wind. Now I was split, with the way he was I could make him suffer—allow him to taste the notorious poison he had concocted. My lips grated open to allow all my frustration out onto his gnarled figure. Yet, I could not. My heart had long forgiven him for all his puppeteering of everyone and now my brain had just caught up. My hand gently touched his arm, reminding him that we were here.

"Dr. Grey, what if I promise you that there will be a place in this world where there will never be color? You can live there, if you want." My voice trailed off, thinking. "You know that place called Antarctica, where there is just snow and penguins? You can live there."

Dr. Grey smiled at me gratefully and, without a word, stalked away to catch the next ride to Antarctica. From that day on, Mrs. Periwinkle could teach us whatever we wanted. Of course, we continued learning math and science. But after that, it was all a little creativity and a step away from a fresh, cheerful day.

Word Choice

Tasslyn Magnusson and Shinjini Samanta focused on the different effects of similar descriptive words in Shinjini's poem, "The Pleasures of Nature."

Dear Reader,

When Shinjini and I met to revise her poem, "The Pleasures of Nature," we talked about words. When we write poems, we use so few words, so they have to do a lot of work and be the best possible words for the ideas we are writing about. It's hard to pick just one, or know which one is the right one.

We started with a line that I loved in her poem. Shinjini wrote, "The flowers sway with glee." This made me smile and imagine nature in a new way. She also wrote "the pearl-blue tears of tremendous joy." I liked that because we often think about tears as from sadness—but then sometimes I have cried when I have been so very happy.

Next, we brainstormed description words. In the first line of her poem, she wrote about "The shining blue sky." We thought of all the possible words that she could use: shining, glistening, sparkling. Shinjini brainstormed so she could have two or three times as many words as she needed.

Then we talked about line breaks. Line breaks are something that pretty much only poets get to use. We get to break the line of words

Whenever

We

Want

TO!

This is really important—see how by putting each word on the line, the reader slows down? I did this in this letter because I want you to see how exciting this poetry tool is. Although Shinjini's lines in her final draft don't break like my example, she has thought about each line and made sure not only were the words the ones she wanted, but she started new lines or ended lines in ways that helped her poem grow.

Using white space effectively is a super tool for poets! You can play with the words and letters on your page and use the space to to shape your ideas. This is about word choice because different words and letters give you different opportunities to play with the space on the page. It is another way poets have to really show their readers the emotions and scenes they are describing in their poems. And when Shinjini played with this idea, it helped her think about her poem in new ways.

In her revision process, Shinjini did something really important. She allowed herself to try. When we talked afterwards, she encouraged writers to just try and have fun. This isn't easy to do. We want our writing to be perfect, and to only come up with ideas we actually will use in our work. Unfortunately, when we focus on perfection, we limit ourselves. A collection of more ideas than we need allows us to pick and choose.

Congratulations to Shinjini on writing, being a poet, and trying!

Tasslyn Magnusson

As a fourth grader, Tasslyn Magnusson once tried to read her school library from A to Z, backwards. She got stuck on P.L. Travers and *Mary Poppins* and has been reading anything and everything since. When she's not writing her poetry or working on her middle grade novels, she's reading fan fiction written by her teens and trading book recommendations with their friends. Tasslyn received her MFA in Writing for Children and Young Adults from Hamline University in January 2017. She has had several poems published and won the 2017 Room Magazine Poetry Prize.

Shinjini Samanta

Shinjini goes to Tru School in Palo Alto, California. She will be in fourth grade this fall. She likes to read, write, and draw. She doesn't have a pet, but really wants a chinchilla! She is currently writing a cause paper about women's education to convince people that women should be allowed to get an education. She really likes to read spy stories, but does not like to play spies anymore. She loves music and listens to different kinds of music.

Tasslyn Magnusson: Do you like to read?
Shinjini Samanta: Yes, I do. I'm like a bookworm!

Q: What is your favorite book?
A: I don't have favorite books, but there are a lot of books I really like. Especially by Laura Ingalls Wilder—*Little House on the Prairie*. I do like A to Z Mysteries by Ron Roy.

Q: Where do you like to write?
A: I usually like taking a pen or pencil and I just scribble down something or start drawing in my room or I go downstairs. I'll do anything on any paper anywhere! My mom says, "If she's not reading, she's writing. If she's not writing, she's drawing."

Q: What changed when you revised?

A: I read over my poem. And I thought about some parts of it. I didn't really like it, and I thought about changing it. I looked at word choice a lot. I just thought about different words until they fit.

Q: What advice do you have for Inklings who might not like to revise?

A: Once I started, I really liked to revise. I found lots of stuff I wanted to change. You can start, you can fix it, keep thinking, work hard! Keep working hard and make sure that the idea you have is good! I liked rewriting the entire poem. I even changed the title!

Q: When did you start writing?

A: There was a contest at our local PBS station and I just wanted to participate. I was five. I thought about the story. It was about Super Why. I drew the pictures, I wrote some of the words, and my mom helped me write the rest of the words. In first grade, I started going to a new school called Tru. At Tru, we do Writer's Studio where everyone gets blank notebooks, even kindergartners. We have to come up with our own stories and write them. First, we just make pictures and then write about them. We start editing for grammar in fourth and fifth grade. In second and third grade, we edit for spelling and meaning.

Q: Why do you enjoy writing?

A: Well, I enjoy writing because I just like it. Since I like reading, I like writing, because I can make things up. Sometimes I get discouraged because it isn't working. What I do is stop writing and go over it and think about what can be next or sometimes I leave that part for later, until I get another idea. I like writing because I can express my imagination and I can write it down in the book.

The Pleasures of Nature

by
Shinjini Samanta

The shining blue sky hovers
over the sparkling sea like a
blanket and it blends into the
feeling of life which spreads
a joyful mood around the
entire world.
When the furious rain clouds flee,
and the sun shows up, the amber
rays of it give a feeling
to me
and make me have
the pearl-blue
tears of tremendous joy.
The flowers sway with
glee as drops of
love shower on
our beautiful Mother Earth.

Specific Details

Dear Reader,

At a high-enough level of abstraction, all stories are the same. The art of telling a story is in the art of choosing and inventing details to distinguish the story that you want to tell from other stories. At the same time, those details are the way you draw your reader into the very universal tale you want to tell them.

From its first draft, Max's story, "By Chance or by Guilt," was a thought-provoking tale about a new person—an Artificial Intelligence, or AI—whose first major emotional contact with life is through the death of the sick man in the AI's care and the AI's subsequent feelings of guilt. To deal with these feelings of guilt, this AI has to leave the place of its first creation and the presence of its designer and enter the wider world. This is a very basic, archetypal, primal sort of story: in some ways, it's like the story of Orestes, or like Eve and Adam in the Garden. One of the challenges with such a story is that it can feel generic. It can feel as if the author is simply showing us a pattern, rather than telling us a story that actually happened . . . or might have happened.

The key to avoiding this pitfall is detail. I'm not talking about the details necessary for the plot, but details beyond what the plot requires. Enough detail makes characters and events feel real. When they feel real, we can relate to them, even though they're different from us. That relatability makes the characters and events feel more universal . . . even as, paradoxically, we have made them actually more specific.

Of course, on the other hand, if you flood your readers with too much detail, they can lose sight of the story and the character.

In my editorial letter, I talked through this issue with Max. On the phone, we discussed a number of possible examples of additional detail that he came up with, and in his revised story, as you can see, he implemented many of them. I think his details make his characters more sympathetic, and they also make the events of "By Chance or by Guilt" feel like real events that might happen to a person. Together, I think these changes added emotional weight and meaning to what was always a great story.

As you're writing your stories, and especially as you are editing, think what details you can add that are not strictly necessary for the plot, but will make your characters and events feel more real.

And keep at it!

Dave Butler

Dave Butler is a lawyer by training, and by day he travels the world as a corporate trainer, teaching business acumen classes. He writes fantasy adventure novels for kids (as Dave Butler) and grown-ups (as D.J. Butler), and he is also acquisitions editor for WordFire Press. When he's home, he likes to study languages, pick the banjo, and play board games with his family.

Max Wang

Max was born in Ontario, Canada, and lived there until he was four, then moved to California, where he currently resides. Max's hobbies include writing short stories and scripts and touring enlarged capitalist cubbies—or, as you might call it, shopping. Max also plays violin and viola; he is currently the concertmaster of his school's chamber orchestra, and a violist in the California Youth Symphony's (CYS) associate orchestra. In the future, Max wants to graduate from UC San Francisco and become a nurse, or even a surgeon, as he's always been interested in biology and relatively good at slapping bandaids on people. In the short term, he wants to run for student council in his freshman year, and although he says it's for leadership, he really just wants to abuse his popularity. Max is looking forward to his summer (actually, parole) and going to high school and its longer lunch periods.

Dave Butler: Your story is written from the point of view of a character who is not human, but an artificial intelligence. What made you interested in writing a story about such a character?

Max Wang: I wanted a story that stood out by using complex emotions that were not traditionally seen in contemporary literature; common emotions for a robot would be love and happiness, like in *The Terminator*. Thus, I created my story by using darker and more complex emotions of humans. This gave me the idea of having an AI, which are thought of as not having human qualities. Some of my inspiration for this was "Flowers for Algernon," which shows a progression of maturity, emotionally and intellectually, by using a journal format. Journals are used by humans to share their most intimate thoughts, but by having a robot do this, it gave the robot human characteristics. Using an AI, I created a plot that would manifest guilt within the robot. Initially, I wanted the robot to stay and perhaps have a happy ending, but I realized that to have the more darker emotions come across, there would have to be more situations that could express these emotions.

Q: You mention that "Flowers for Algernon" helped inspire this story. What are some novels that you find especially inspiring or important to you?
A: Apart from "Flowers for Algernon," some novels that helped inspire me and taught me something were *The Count of Monte Cristo*, *Ender's Game*, and *Speaker for the Dead*. *The Count of Monte Cristo* inspired me to have greater emotional depth within my story, using the characters to show isolation and alienation. *Ender's Game* and *Speaker for the Dead* also showed isolation through the main character, but also strong feelings of guilt. It also helped through its use of alien characters, who were drastically different and naturally showed the rift between human and any other species, contributing to the difference between the robot and Jorge.

Q: In addition to being a writer, you're a musician. What similarities do you find between writing and playing music? What differences?
A: They were both creative outlets for me to express myself. I really enjoy these two things, and they help take my mind off of other subjects, such as school. The difference between the two, however, is that while writing is more peaceful and relaxed, playing music is more intense and can be tiring physically, while writing can be tiring mentally.

Q: What did you find the most enjoyable thing about writing this story? What was the most challenging thing?
A: To be honest, the most enjoyable thing about writing this story was the excitement and joy of having it published. Of course, I enjoyed the calming sessions of writing, but at that moment, I was the happiest. The most challenging thing was probably coming up with such an idea, as I went through many rough drafts and concepts before settling on writing this story. It was also a little stressing, as well as tiring, to write so much, but I think it was worth it in the end, to see my story being published and having my ego inflate just a little bit (it's actually larger than a hot air balloon now).

By Chance or by Guilt

by
Max Wang

March 22

I do not know how it happened, but with a jolt, I came to be. I faced a middle-aged man, slightly wrinkled. He was inspecting me. To my left was an old car, and to the other side was the wall, just two feet away. It was a garage. He explained that I had been created by him. His name was Jorge. That is all I know about myself. Jorge is a very nice man. Later, he would send me to stay at his father's house, and keep a journal so he could see what was happening. Jorge told me to care for his father, Lucio. Lucio is also very kind, but he forgets many things. I learned more about Jorge's wife Catalina today. I had seen her once, in the hospital. She was smiling. I didn't see her after. Lucio said that she was very proud of Jorge and me, and he stopped there. Jorge told me it would be good for him if I kept writing about what happened today, so that is all I will write. My instructions from Jorge are to monitor Lucio's vitals, so I do, and he is fine.

March 27

When Lucio woke up today, I asked him how he was feeling. He said he was fine, but his heart rate was faster, but not dangerous. I notified Jorge. He visited soon afterward, but he didn't stay for long. He made sure that his father was fine, then looked at me for a while. He had his hand on his chin, like he was forgetting something. Forgetfulness may run in the family.

March 29

Lucio seems to have worsening memory. He can't remember what he is doing, and today, he did not know what I was doing here. That is all I did for him. I have made sure his needs are set. Jorge has also told me to give him these pills lately. He says it will help with the memory issues.

April 2

Today, when Jorge visited, he told me to buy groceries. He gave me some money and instructions on where to go. It was my first time walking out of the house. Outside, it is very different. I saw many people. All of them look different. A lot of people stared at me, and they seemed confused. I reached the store. I picked out what Jorge had on his list. Some of them asked me what I was doing there. One of them called me tin can, and asked me to buy some dog food for the wild dog in the alleyway. I didn't get it, but I smiled anyway because they were laughing. My body is not made out of tin, so I do not know why they would call me that. Regardless, I bought some dog food. Money had never been a problem with Jorge for as long as I could remember. I walked out, and passed the alleyway. The dog started barking wildly, yapping and howling. I brought out the bag of food. I spilled some into my hand, and stretched it out to the dog. It approached me warily, and knocked my hand away with its muzzle. I poured some more and left it on the pavement. The dog approached me once more. I backed away, and it started devouring the food. I emptied the bag. Once there was no more food left, it gave a soft bark, and ran back down the alley.

The streets were still new to me, but I still had the map, and so after a while, I found my way back. Jorge opened the door for me, and then left.

April 3

Today, Jorge came to see us earlier than he had mentioned. I was surprised to see him at the doorstep. He said he wanted to talk to me, so I stepped outside. He said that he needed me to pick up a package from his friend who had been developing robotic parts while he was at the lab for a meeting. He needed them for a very important project. I nodded my head. I could help. He said that Lucio's vitals had to be fine before I left, and gave me the instructions. Then he went in, checked in on him, and left. Finally, an opportunity to prove that I was useful.

April 4

I unplugged myself from my charging outlet, and I woke up Lucio. He was frowning. He said something, but I could not pick up on what he was saying, so I took his vitals in case anything was wrong. It was all

fine. He was most likely tired. I brought him a glass of water, in case he wanted it. He seemed to be resting now. With everything fine, I walked out and followed the route to Jorge's friend's house. It took me quite a while, and some people shouted things at me. I turned to them, and nodded. I didn't understand what they were saying. It did not make sense, again. Once I arrived at Jorge's friend's house, I rang the doorbell. He invited me in, so I walked into his living room. He said he was quite amazed. He tested how well I heard, and had me reply to some things he said. He slowly nodded his head, but then cocked his head slightly. He said the package would help me become even more helpful, and handed it to me. I thanked him and left. On the way back, I got a little bit lost, so I retraced my steps and found my way back to the house. When I arrived, I saw a large red vehicle parked by the door. They were wheeling out someone.

April 7

Jorge told me what happened today. The strange things that had been happening to his father were symptoms of something called a stroke. I did not know what that was. I had only checked his vitals, which were fine. Jorge said it wasn't my fault. He had his head in his palms, and was muttering things under his breath. After a while, Jorge told me to go into the car, and we drove to the hospital.

April 14

Today, I attended the funeral for Lucio. It was raining that day. I got a little bit soaked. It was a different sensation. There were not a lot of people there. Some relatives and friends were there, and talked about how Lucio was a very kind man. They were all very nice, but some people looked at me when the speaker talked about Jorge. They looked away quickly, and turned to Jorge. After the funeral ended, I didn't want to go back. I told Jorge I was going to buy some groceries. We could use a bit more, but I wanted to visit the dog again. I bought some more dog food, and a small bed with an overhang. I didn't want the dog to be cold and hungry, but when I got to the same alleyway, the dog wasn't there. A man passed me. I recognized him as the one who called me tin can. He asked me if I was looking for the dog, and I nodded. He said that it was long gone. The pound had come to take its body away. He offered to take the food and bed to a nearby shelter. I handed them over to him.

April 17

These days, Jorge has stayed at Lucio's house. He has stayed in his room, and does not come out often. He is occupied with studying the package that I have brought him, and sometimes asks me to show him my processing chip. I do not know what he is doing, but he says it is very important.

April 20

Jorge asked me today to come with him to the lab. On the drive there, he said that it was for an important project that he was doing. He said that he did not want to reveal much right now, but it would involve me. We got there, and he set up this lab while I waited. He told me then to open my panel, unlock everything, and to turn off. He said to trust him. I did that.

April 21

I woke up in the house. Jorge asked me how I was doing, and I said I felt a little weird, but fine. I asked him what he had done at the lab. Jorge was a little surprised. It seemed like he was thinking. Then, he said that he had improved my circuits, and that he wanted me to start learning. He went into his room, and found a pile of books. He said they were about artificial intelligence and robots. He wanted me to read them.

April 28

It has been a week. I've scanned and processed all the books. It was quite interesting. The books gave me a lot of useful information that accounted for the history and how the AI were developed. It described how computing chips were made, and how scientists were trying to make them able to be self-aware. When Jorge had seen that I had finished them, he sat down at my desk. He asked me what I had learned, and I replied that the books were about A.I. He nodded. He said that I was an artificial intelligence in a robot. I was the first robot to successfully become self-aware. Jorge said that he had made robots that were capable of responding, but not thinking. He said that I could think now, but I don't know how to think. I didn't think of that.

May 3

Jorge came into my room today, and sat down. He started talking about Catalina. He told me that he had wanted a son, but couldn't. I didn't question him, so he went on. They had tried for years, but eventually, they had given up, gotten old. Catalina had gotten sick a year later, and the bills were expensive, and Jorge needed money. He had started experimenting with his work, and had successfully created me, like he had told me. That was what I remembered, but I didn't realize why Jorge was doing this. Now, he had told me.

May 5

As I browsed through the books and articles in the house and on the Internet, I began to have questions. I realized that Jorge had been staying inside because of his grief for Lucio, Catalina, and me. And for some reason, I had only just noticed. I opened up a document online, and began to type a letter. It wasn't for anybody, but I felt that it could be important later.

> *Jorge had successfully created a sentient robot, and he had used his invention to care for his ill father. But the robot wasn't smart enough. Perhaps it had been his orders, and maybe it was the robot itself. But the robot wasn't a human. It wasn't good enough. Eventually, his father passed away, but in a way that could have been easily prevented. He hadn't been with his father. The old man had passed away alone, and in a sense, I was responsible. My case didn't help, either. His family must have blamed him for creating a robot to take care of his duties. And if I had been smart enough, this whole thing wouldn't have happened. And if it had happened a week later, I would have been able to notice what was happening. With this, Jorge had lost his only family.*

I had not realized that Lucio was in a dangerous situation. I could process what was happening, but to me, he was fine. His vitals were fine, but it didn't mean he was fine. Was it my fault then, if I didn't know any better? Would it have been Jorge's fault? Should I have notified Jorge? The book Jorge gave me said that the robots before me all operated on human commands, but even so, I didn't notify Jorge when his father was experiencing the symptoms of a stroke.

May 6

Jorge doesn't visit anymore. I think it is because he doesn't want to see me, or this house. The last time he visited, he didn't stay for long, and told me to get a job. He said that there were some openings at the nearby store. I went online and checked for some jobs, and scheduled a time for an interview. I feel like Jorge is telling me to move on, but I don't think he even has recovered from the loss yet. I'm not too sure I am, either.

May 8

I decided to walk to the library with the map I found online, and I checked out some books. I had trouble trying to read the books that I checked out.. I keep on asking myself the same question. Could I have done anything better? Should I even put others to blame? I can never be too sure of my answer, no matter how much I ponder it over. If only, if only. Life's unfair.

May 9

I didn't get the job. The manager thinks I'll scare away the customers.

They think that in the future, robots will take all of their human jobs. But from what I know, I am one of a kind. Unless, of course, Jorge decides to implement the technology used for me into the other robots. But right now, the other robots aren't a threat to anybody. The hardly do anything apart from what their programming tells them to. I guess I'll stay at home then.

June 23

I've taken a break from logging every week or so. The past month, I've spent my time gathering my thoughts, and reading. The books have really taught me a thing or two. Humans are quite talented at telling stories, in fact. But I noticed that they're really something much more than that. They have messages within them, and the story revolves around it. The messages are timeless, and are like snippets of advice that are found by telling a story. Nothing has happened outside. Jorge hasn't visited. I'm quite sure that he's lost the reason to visit. The place reminds him too much of his father. It's been a while, and I've come to accept the fact that Lucio's death, while it could have been prevented, could not have gone any other way. Life was intended for it to be so. Still, I couldn't stop dwelling on the fact that I had left Lucio on his deathbed. It bothered me, that I could have saved him. No matter how extenuating the circumstances were, I couldn't help but feel guilty.

July 6

I've decided to take some breaks from Lucio's house, but I have to charge my batteries every night. I did some research about a portable

energy source. It recommended solar panels to me, and I decided to try to make some. I don't want to be chained to the house. I want to leave, but what would happen with Jorge? I am his creation, and his son, in a sense. I must mean a lot to him.

July 28

I finished my solar panel, and it works. I've decided that I have to leave. For the sake of Jorge and his family, I think it is for the best that I leave. To everybody else, I am a constant reminder of what happened on that day. It causes nothing to Jorge but wounded pride, and guilt. I, too feel guilty, but I am directly responsible for what happened, and I do not have any attachments to this town. I have built a solar panel so I don't run out of electricity, and apart from that, I need nothing else. I left the computer after I decided to integrate the internet into my memory. I left everything else the same, but I took the letter that I had written nearly three months ago, and continued it on the back.

> *Jorge,*
>
> *While we are still caught up in the events that happened on that miserable day, I have come to accept the fact that yes, it was something easily preventable, but it is not you, nor I, who is directly responsible. Rather, it was the accumulation of us two, and the miracle that we call life, that I feel so lucky to have been a part of. Life moves on, and so should you. I wish that you would forgive me one day. Eventually, you will find your destination. But for me, I feel that it is the end of the road, at least in this town. I think it is best for me to leave, lest I remind you of what happened. In a sense, I'm not truly satisfied; I have*

made it my goal to find something that is greater than humans and robots, something that we can look at and see it for what it truly is, and hopefully it will be free from the flaws that scar us. I hope this is the case for me, and I wish you the best of luck in your own life. I know how much you've gone through, and I hope to come back one day. But as of now, it is time for my own journey.

I read it over, folded the letter, and placed it in the mailbox. Then, I set off.

Tone to Build Tension

Dear Reader,

Often, when someone writes a poem, they are expressing a feeling or attitude about a subject. This is sometimes called the tone of the poem. The poet doesn't always think about the best way to say something—they let their feelings take the lead. This is an important step in writing poetry, because it is a way of expressing our deepest feelings. After that first draft, a poet will often look again at the words and phrases they've used, to see if these are the best ones to convey what they want to say.

When Anna and I revised her poem, "Phoenix," we looked at picking the best words to make the tone of the poem stronger. It was clear that she had deep feelings about the fire which consumed a neighborhood. Here are some of the words she used to describe the fire and its effects: "tears crowded the edges of my eyes," "trees crumble," "horrendous flames," "the sun dyeing the white clouds," "flames licking the shores," "no limit to the power…"

Anna had read about the terrible fires in California that destroyed lands, forests, and homes. She had an opportunity to sit by a still lake and imagine what it must feel like to be one of the people who'd lost a home. And it was with these feelings that she wrote the poem. In "Phoenix," there is a sense of helplessness and hopelessness in the first half of the poem. The poet is trying to deal with the enormity and ferocity of this event. It overwhelms her.

In the second half of the poem, there is a different tone. The damage is done, and there is sadness and loss. The poet relives memories of what life was like before the fire. But there is also a quiet peace as she wanders amongst the ashes and damage. And finally, there is hope as new signs of life emerge (the tiny green seedling). Amidst the devastation, life goes on. Life wins in the end, like a phoenix rising from the ashes.

First, in her revision, Anna found strong verbs and adjectives to better convey these changing emotions. She already had some wonderful similes and metaphors. Strong words help bring out the rise and fall of tension in the poem. In our conversations, we questioned why she had chosen particular words and whether these words showed the reader how she really felt in the moment.

Second, we looked at the characters in her poem: the poet (who was watching and despairing), and the fire itself. We talked about the fire's journey of destruction, and how that made the poet feel at every stage. We also looked at the words and phrases chosen to show that journey.

In this poem, the fire has a mind of its own. It's a thinking being, determined to win this "fight." This made the fire all the more frightening. In an early draft, Anna chose to have the fire hesitate, to be stopped by the edge of the lake. At the same time, the poet's emotions were increasing in fear and tension as she watched the fire advance. During revision, we talked about how that moment seemed to cut back the fire's power, which didn't match the rising emotions of the poet. Anna decided that the fire should not be held back. In the revision, she allowed the flames to push

...with all their might.
I saw no limit to the power,
The strength,
The persistence.

In the revised version, the flames were like a powerful army consuming everything in their path. This matched the poet's action of stumbling backward and running away. It also contrasted much more with the quiet in the second half, after the fight had seemingly been lost. In this version, the tension goes up so much higher, and the loss seems so much greater. (But only for a while).

The next time you write a poem, think about how you feel about the subject, and how the words you are choosing make those emotions come through more clearly or with more power. Pick a word or phrase and then brainstorm as many ways as possible to express it differently. Choose the best ones. Don't be afraid to make changes. You can always go back to the original if none of the other changes work. Play with your work until it feels just right.

Happy writing,
Ailynn Knox-Collins

Ailynn Knox-Collins loves to read poetry and writes mostly about spaceships, strange new worlds, and aliens. Sometimes, she writes about boarding school magic and ghosts, too. She is working on several novels, and a graphic novel. She has published a series of middle grade novels about a girl who moves to Mars, in the far-off future, called Redworld. When she's not reading or writing, Ailynn is walking her four big dogs, or partnering with one of them, an Old English Sheepdog named Lady Rose, as a therapy team with Reading with Rover. She and Lady Rose love to listen to kids read to them at libraries and schools around Seattle.

Anna Yang

Anna is a teen who loves to write poetry. In her free time, she enjoys playing volleyball, spending time with friends, drawing, and reading mystery novels. Her favorite books include *The Forgotten Garden* by Kate Morton and *Murder on the Orient Express* by Agatha Christie. When she's not reading, she enjoys learning about the human brain and how it works.

Ailynn Knox-Collins: What changed in your poem as you revised for tone?
Anna Yang: I made the fire seem stronger, like it was alive. I added a sense of hopelessness like there was nothing she could do about it. She wasn't in control.

Q: What advice do you have for other Inklings who might not like to revise their poems?
A: I think that revising is really important because there can be mistakes that you made that can make the poem not how you would want it to go. Revising can change that and make it a lot more powerful.

Q: Do you like to read? Poetry or prose? What are your favorite genres?
A: I like to read both. I feel like poetry is different because there are a lot of ways you can interpret poetry and lots of people have different interpretations of what the author is trying to tell you. I like murder mysteries and action stories.

Q: Do you write murder mysteries?
A: No.

Q: Do you write a lot of poetry?
A: Yes, when I have time. I write a lot for contests. I've won a contest once and my poem was submitted to a magazine.

Q: What does it feel like when you see your name in print?
A: I I feel like I actually got something done and it was worth my time and effort to do it.

Q: How do you come up with ideas for your poems?
A: I first think of a place and what emotions come to me when I imagine myself in that place and I just write about that. And I come up with a story that goes with that place. In writing "Phoenix," I was in Monterey, standing across a lake. There are a lot of forest fires in California now and I was thinking about how someone would react to their home being lost in a fire.

Q: Do you enjoy sharing your poetry? With whom?
A: Yes. I feel like a lot of people can relate to my poetry. If not, they can experience it through the descriptions in my poetry.

Q: What are you writing next?
A: Now I'm working on a poem about the ocean. We have a writing club at my school and my teacher invited me to write a poem for their magazine. It's an online website that will be opened next week or soon. I came up with the idea in the car. Sometimes I look at the sky and it reminds me of the ocean, so I decided to write about it.

Q: What are your long-term plans?
A: I might put together an anthology. I don't think I'd be successful with prose because I like to describe things and in prose, I'd need a giant plot. I'm not sure I have enough ideas for that.

Phoenix

by

Anna Yang

I stood before the still lake,
looking across water, only to find more water;
tears crowded the edges of my eyes
threatening to spill any time.
My eyes fell to my hands,
the only thing I seemed to be in

      control
           of.

I looked up to see the trees crumble,
bowing down to the horrendous flames
the color of fall leaves, bursts
of yellow and orange, crushing
everything underneath.
The sky was on fire too;
the sun dyeing the white clouds
first pink, then purple, then hints of bright red;
just the edge of the horizon at first,

but the colors took

      control,

                like
ink seeping through paper.
Like the sun etching history
into the clouds,
Leaving the past for only the birds to read
and for me to remember.

I saw my home,
my life,
the animals who dug up my backyard plants,
all disappearing with the crackle of the fire.
I saw the flames licking the shores of the lake,
pushing with all their might.
I saw no limit to the power,
the strength,
the persistence.

They advanced as a
single
being working for a same goal:
to destroy.

I stumbled backwards from the fire
miles away,
my head dizzy from the
strong smoke fumes.
I lay onto the grass and closed my eyes.

    This won't last forever.

Nothing does,
I reminded myself.

I walk alongside the fallen trees,
a path paved by the thousands of feet
that have already come to mourn the loss
of this natural majesty.
I kneel down
to honor the place I once found a
tiny bird,
almost frozen from the winter cold.
If I shut out the rest of the world,
I can almost hear its melodious voice
serenading me.
I reach down to pick up a golden leaf,
admiring the rough beauty
before it falls apart to ash,
blown away by the wind.
Through the scattered piles of burnt wood and leaves,
I find a green seedling,
shooting up from the destruction.
The hope within me

     rekindles,

and I know that if one seed can grow,
the whole forest can be rebuilt again,

    As a phoenix rising from the ashes.

Specific vs. Abstract Language

Helen Pyne worked with Allison Gable to illustrate intense emotions through specific details in Allison's story, "Spring."

Dear Reader,

In "Spring," Allison used eloquent, poetic prose to write about the powerful emotions associated with romantic love and the heart-wrenching pain of loss. Her well-crafted sentences, marvelous metaphors, and ear for rhythm and cadence captivated me immediately. Narrated from a third person point of view, "Spring" takes place entirely inside the head of a single, unnamed character as she walks through a park, trying to sort out her tumultuous feelings. The character is brokenhearted and unbearably sad because she's just ended a relationship with the boy she loved. Her thoughts and memories are a meditation on the grief and loss she feels.

This narration choice brought with it certain challenges. Initially, there was very little story action—no dialogue or character interaction happening in scene, since the tale is told solely through her reflections. Allison did a good job of telling us how the main character felt, but the emotions she described were abstract concepts. I didn't just want to hear that the protagonist was angry or lonely; I wanted to see specific examples of what triggered these intense emotions so I could understand how and why she'd come to feel that way. What did the boy do to hurt her, for instance? What were the "upsetting comments" he made? And most importantly, what made the narrator fall in love with him in the first place? Was there a way to show readers the joy she experienced as well as the depression that derailed her? This question gave us our revision focus: to flesh out the narrator's vague thoughts with specific, concrete details.

To do this, Allison generated new material using sensory language that evoked images and associations in the reader's head. As she began to add specific anecdotes and lines of dialogue into the story, the characters became increasingly vivid and real. The white roses the boy gave her, the pillow fort they built, and the descriptions of the warm-weather activities the couple enjoyed helped us understand what sparked their love. Then, Allison contrasted these good times with their snarky dialogue, a snowy, barren landscape, and the boy's abusive behavior to illustrate the sad deterioration of their relationship.

We made the time frame more specific, too. To follow a story, readers need to understand specifically when events happened. In the original version, it was unclear to me how long the couple had dated before things began falling apart. When I asked Allison about this, she didn't know how long they'd dated, either! Like many writers, she'd begun the story with only a vague idea and then discovered her protagonist's personality and journey as she wrote. It's not uncommon, of course, for writers to discover new story elements and errors in later drafts. Sometimes we don't have a chance to check for logic and consistency until revision is well underway. Allison went back and cemented the relationship timeframe so that her characters' breakup would occur just before spring. That way, the title, "Spring," could have several layers of meaning. While the story takes place in the season of spring (note the specific reference to cherry blossom trees), it also reflects the narrator's emotional growth and blossoming, new perspective.

I admired the way Allison took the heartfelt emotions explored in the story and elevated and enhanced them with specific, concrete details. Her narrator's insights and articulate observations make this a compelling story of character transformation.

Helen Pyne

Helen Pyne has worked as a children's book editor in New York City and currently writes, edits, and teaches creative writing classes in the Bay Area. Her published work includes magazine articles and two novels in a mystery series for kids. The mother of four children, she loves to hike, travel, and cook. With an MFA in Writing for Children and Young Adults from Vermont College of Fine Arts, she blogs with other professional writers at *www.throughthetollbooth.com*. She's taught writing workshops in foreign countries like Mexico and Kenya and believes in the power of a good story to unite people.

Allison Gable

Allison is a freshman at Amador Valley. She plays trombone in her school's concert band and is learning ukulele at home. Her family has a fox red lab and two cats, one black and one gray. She also loves chocolate, especially brownies, and wishes she could sing.

Helen Pyne: What was the most challenging part of the revision process for you? Did the final draft of your story turn out the way you expected?
Allison Gable: The most challenging part was keeping the flow of the story when adding new material or revising. Sometimes things would end up working on their own but then I would have to change them more to have them fit in with the direction of the whole story. As for the finished product, I didn't really have a vision of how it would change when I submitted it, but I'm happy it turned out the way it did.

Q: How did you go about replacing abstract concepts with specific descriptions? Did your story change when you did this?
A: First, I had to think about the characters' relationship and what actually happened. Having a consistent timeline and a better idea of the actual events in my mind helped me come up with the smaller scenes and images inside of them. When I did this, the arc of my story became less directed by the narrator's thoughts and more by the reader's interpretations of what happened.

Q: Where do you find your story ideas?
A: A lot of the time, my ideas stem from a combination of images in my mind of a character or scene and restless late-night brainstorming. I might be influenced by a book I like or a post I saw online. For this story,

there was just a vaguely poetic image in my head, and I remember just kind of describing it and then writing from there.

Q: What do you do if you're stuck?

A: If I'm stuck because a specific part of the story doesn't feel right, often I'll just leave the document and come back to it later to reread before I start to write again. Seeing the bigger picture and refreshing the context of a specific piece can help it make more sense in my head. I can also get new ideas from things I'd forgotten I'd written.

Q: When did you first start writing fiction? When, where and how often do you usually write?

A: I started writing in fifth grade, a fantasy story that I wrote with a friend. It didn't get very far, so the first time I actually finished a creative writing project was in eighth grade. Now I usually write on my laptop at home, and most of the time I start later at night than I should. When I was working on my most recent long-term project, I didn't write on a very consistent schedule, either—it depended on what section of the story I was writing and how exciting that part of the plot was to me.

Q: What do you enjoy most about writing?

A: I like that it's a way to create something you're passionate about—instead of wanting to live inside of some other artist's world, you can create your own. You can have characters that you love and develop, and you get to describe places that are only in your head. You get to hurt the people in your story and watch them break but then watch them stand back up and face their fears.

Q: Do you have any advice for other young writers?

A: Just keep writing. You might look back at what you've written and think it's really bad, but that means you've gotten better. Also, don't worry about making things perfect—if you're writing a rough draft, it's not going to be your final product. You need to shape your story first before you can refine all the details.

Spring

by

Allison Gable

She walks among flowers. Light pink blossoms scattering in the wind, gossamer petals catching in her short hair. Dark branches hold them up, steady, calm as the breeze dances around them. Strong. ~~Like the arms that left, leaving her alone with their lingering cold~~. She pushes back her memories and feels the wind dying down, relishing it as if the flood of warmth could reach inside of her and rekindle the fire.

Dozens of street lamps glow along the sides of the paneled pavement, stretching out into the distance, lighting up the park even though the sun is only beginning to set and she can see just fine. And even if she couldn't, the path is familiar enough to her that she could find her way to her usual bench in the dark.

The thirteenth lamp. Marked with names and symbols scratched into the paint, a collage that matches the other lampposts in its messy patterns and peeling edges. But it's different, because it's hers. She's sat here every day she's come, even when people left and

the seasons faded in and out. A living portrait of weathered tranquility, much better than anything she could ever paint. It's her favorite place for drawing and she'd come here whenever she felt like letting her worries go, like white dandelion tufts in the wind.

She looks up, past the R+N circled with a heart and the *Ari was here* in jagged letters that she's grown so accustomed to seeing. To take her mind off of everything, she tries to focus on the trees. The trees she's climbed countless times, sitting in their branches with different cameras, trying to capture the world in a box. The trees that have finally begun to bloom now that the seasons have changed, like a card turned over to reveal a suit of pink spades. The trees that reach towards the sky, making her feel small. ~~So small; she's nothing without him.~~ She tries to fight her thoughts, to concentrate on something else. ~~But she wasn't anything with him, either. That was something he never let her forget.~~

She sinks backward, her eyes pressed shut, cutting off the bad memories with good ones. A flash of scissors through the reel of film. Another scene slapped on with glue.

She remembers it like yesterday—how he was so kind and strong. How hearing his voice never got old. After a long day, it was so refreshing, like a breeze on a hot afternoon, ice in a drink. Arms that wrapped around her in the morning when they met up for coffee. A smile that could make her trip over her own feet, blushing as red as her hair after she'd dyed it in September. A laugh that could erase her doubts if only for a moment that they were in love. That she loved him. That he loved her. It was happiness. It was . . . bliss.

It was lying in the middle of their college quad in the fall, running their fingers through the grass, getting leaves caught in their hair and soaking in the colors around them. It was the smell of old textbooks and coffee-stained pages. It was a safety net, being tangled up in pink cheeks and secret looks, knowing that wherever life took them, they'd have each other.

~~It was gone.~~

Her breath is unsteady as she opens her eyes. She finds that her hair has fallen around her face, a parted veil. No longer red but brown. She tucks it behind her ears and looks down at the black sketchbook in her hands, brushing her thumb across the worn paper cover and focusing on the familiar texture.

It takes more energy than it should to flip through the pages of old, messy art and find somewhere new. She comes to a blank page and slips her pencil out from where it's tucked into the spiral. When she starts drawing, there is no wave of inspiration. That spark has been getting harder and harder to find. But she makes herself start with a simple circle, the outline rough but at least not lopsided. She builds off of the shape with a cross, a line, a jaw. Ears, eyes, lips, a nose. It's nothing special, an outline of a girl's face. Though it looks bland–she hasn't drawn much else in the past few months, feeling a pit where her confidence should be.

As she draws, night descends around her. Suddenly the light from the street lamp is the only thing keeping her afloat in the dark sea, a bubble universe of light in the sleeping park. The whir of engines and faraway sounds of loud music drift over from nearby traffic, but she pays no attention. She's alone with her thoughts.

His eyes were brown, warm then cold. ~~The things he'd said: "Crybaby." "It's cute how you think you're so talented." She'd watched as he took the piece of paper from when they first met, the one she'd~~

~~excitedly scribbled her phone number on, and crumpled it in his clenched fist. Like that day in June when they'd met at the subway station had meant nothing.~~

But he kept coming around. *"I love you."*

~~And she'd yelled that it was no excuse for what he did.~~ Was it? Either way, it was too late. The past winter had cast them so far apart, stranding her in a cycle of picking up the phone and convincing herself to put it back down. ~~The cold, familiar presence of his hand in hers is long gone.~~

Now her hands are warm, her fingertips silvery from smudging the lead. It's familiar in a different way. New, but old. It feels…like her. But it's a her without him.

She doesn't know how to feel.

She flips the pencil and erases a piece of the hair she drew wrong, then tries drawing it again. If only she could do the same with the scenes in her memories. Make things turn out right, if that would have been possible. Could there have been a happy ending? Maybe if she'd said something else, done something differently, she wouldn't have ended up with a broken heart.

They'd gone for a weekend to their local summer picnic place, except it was January and covered in snow. Their oversized boots stomping through the white blanket, their hands shoved in their pockets. She'd tried to think of something to say but couldn't. The atmosphere was so *wrong*—no laughing families, no smells of lake water and rosemary chicken on the grill, no smoke blowing into the pine trees above her head. Instead she was stuck with wet socks and numb toes, the world around her lifeless and so white her eyes hurt. It wasn't the same place she'd fallen in love with back then.

After too many long minutes of silence, he finally spoke. "This is a pretty thick layer of snow, huh?" He kicked at it halfheartedly. "I'm surprised we even made it here."

She looked down, away from him. "With your car?" she said. "I'm surprised we got out of the driveway at all."

❀

Snap—the lead breaks off and the stub of the pencil hits the paper with a grating scratch. The sketchbook is suddenly useless. She breathes in, lost. Confused. And so she tucks it under her arm, stands up, and starts walking.

Where am I going?

Away.

Even in the dark, her boots know the feel of the sidewalk. They know where to go. And she's aware of where the pomegranate tree is, tucked away behind the maintenance shed in the south corner, but she's surprised anyway when she ends up there somehow.

It still looks just like it did in her photographs. A little taller than her, with green leaves and dark reddish-pink fruit half eaten by bugs. Those dry, empty husks are the only things hanging now, but in the summer there would be a few good ones. Full and ripe, with enough juice to be enjoyable. They'd found one of these rare pomegranates last July, sitting under the tree with its smell of soil and summer leaves, cracking the fruit open with their bare hands and popping the seeds into their mouths. Laughing. It had tasted tart and rich and good. He had . . .

253

She realizes she's crying.

The tears are hot, the air around her cold—and suddenly she's turning back. Some part of her had wanted just a taste of those times, but it hurts too much. His absence is still too fresh. She walks with her head down, shoulders shaking and sobs caught in her throat. There's no stopping the memories anymore.

Numbly, she reminisces about everything she'd had—everything they'd had. The white roses on their first date, the ones she'd kept in the glass even after they died because she hadn't wanted to throw them away. Going back to community college in the fall, visiting each other's houses, sharing notes and watching movies. Cuddling on freezing cold nights, cheering each other up during midterms by texting silly messages back and forth.

She'd felt something off about the relationship after they'd met up during winter break, a few days before Christmas. She'd hid the notion underneath their piles of blankets in her living room pillow fort, tossing another marshmallow into his mouth and laughing when his bounced off her nose. But after New Year's, it felt like she was walking on eggshells, wondering when he'd laugh at her drawings or call her *nobody* again and her feet would get cut. It had taken more than a few scars before she finally decided to confront him.

March 20th. She had been shaking, trying to explain everything she'd felt, and he didn't even say a word.

Until he looked up. *"So you want to leave me?"*

Her eyes widened. *"That wasn't what I was saying…"*

"So you think you can walk on your own? You need me just as much as I need you." A pause. *"Suki,* I need you.*"*

"I didn't mean . . . I—"

He laughed. *"Of course you didn't, did you. Because you haven't meant any of this since day one. You were just acting the part so you could feel better, to pretend—"*

"I just wanted love."

"You want love? Really? Well, I'm the only one who will love you. And right now, you're not doing very much to make yourself lovable." She thought that he would storm off into the next room to shatter something against the wall like before.

Instead, there was a flash of red in her vision as he slapped her.

She couldn't breathe, couldn't look away. Everything fell dead still.

She'd realized then it was time to end whatever they had. It had killed her to face him and stand her ground, to not give in to his pleas of *I love you*. She'd cried, then and for hours afterwards. But he had cried, too, and so she'd yelled at herself for being a horrible person.

That had been almost a month ago. At least for now, the tears have stopped. Still, every time she thinks of it, a horrible feeling grows in her stomach. Twisting.

That day she'd done the hardest thing she'd ever had to do.

But . . .

But it had been right.

She looks up at the moon—full in the night sky, though it is overshadowed by the cherry blossom trees—and finally understands that the presence she'd been wanting to feel by her side wasn't him. It was the idea of him, the him before he'd started hurting her. The him that wasn't coming back.

No more cold silence. No more constant reminders of how little she's worth. No more slaps, then *I'm sorry*s and forced reconciliation.

Now she can put back together what he's broken in her and take time to heal. She can find her way back.

She still misses him. But she has missed herself more.

She smiles at the full moon and takes another shaky step forward.

She walks among her demons.

Alone, done with trying to forget.

Beautiful, like the flowers on the trees; a watercolor spirit searching for the color of hope.

But though her heart is filled with rain, she is strong.

She is whole.

~~He was winter.~~

She is spring.

Plot and Pacing

Joanna Ho Bradshaw and Ember Summer worked to strengthen the story arc with good pacing in Ember's story, "Three Gnomes and a Crow."

Dear Reader,

Increasing tension, developing characters, and raising stakes are just a few aspects of storytelling impacted by a strong, well-paced plot. Plot and pacing are skills that even the most experienced writers struggle to get just right. When Ember and I met, we worked on two aspects of plot and pacing.

In her original draft, Ember's story reached its climax as a predatory crow grabbed the main character's younger brother. This predator was introduced about two thirds of the way through the story, and the conflict was resolved several sentences later.

We brainstormed ways she might begin building tension earlier: Could she introduce the predator towards the beginning? Might she use foreshadowing to create a sense of rising conflict? Ember planted seeds throughout her story to generate tension and speed up the pacing. She made small, thoughtful tweaks and added well-placed details that completely altered the arc of her story.

Ember and I also brainstormed new possibilities for resolving the main conflict of her story. In the first draft, the main characters are saved from the crow by a wolf. We discussed ways the main characters might solve their own problems, and thus become the heroes of their own story. In the end, Ember decided that the main characters would . . .

Just kidding! Not going to ruin the ending for you; you'll have to read the story to see what happens!

Like Ember, you can revise your work by asking yourself questions like these:

- How might I build tension from the beginning of my story?
- How might the main character(s) solve their problems?
- How can the plot reveal more about my characters?
- How can I increase the stakes of my story?

As you ask yourself these questions, you may find yourself rewriting entire sections of your story. Or, like Ember, you may find subtle ways—a new sentence here, a phrase there—to bring out new dimensions of your work.

Happy writing,

Joanna Ho Bradshaw

Joanna Ho Bradshaw is the Lead Professional Development Designer for Ready to Run PD at Nearpod. She creates workshops to teach teachers how to teach. She has been a classroom teacher, administrator, and school designer. A graduate of UPenn, she holds a Master's degree in education from the Principal Leadership Institute at the University of California, Berkeley . . . though she has no idea where her diplomas are currently located. She writes picture books and YA, and believes deeply in the need for more diverse representation in children's books. Joanna loves chocolate chip cookies and impromptu dance parties. She has two children, ages three and one.

Ember Summer

Ember is thirteen years old and was published in a book compiled by her sixth grade teacher. She enjoys reading, and would be hard pressed to say what her favorite book is (probably a tie between Narnia, *Anne of Green Gables*, Harry Potter, and the Inheritance Cycle). She loves all things animal, and plans to become a veterinarian when she grows up, after she becomes a world famous author. She currently lives in Portland, Oregon with her mother, father, and a younger brother (her Sovan inspiration).

Joanna Ho Bradshaw: When did you start writing and why?
Ember Summer: I started writing when I was about eight because I'd told myself stories for as long as I can remember and I wanted to write them down.

Q: Where do your story ideas come from?
A: I get my ideas from stories I tell myself or based on my everyday experiences.

Q: What do you do when you get stuck?
A: When I get stuck, I leave my story until I feel like I want to write more, and then I come back.

Q: What changed in your story when you revised to increase tension in the plot?

A: When I changed my story, I added some foreshadowing, and bulked up the "fight scene."

Q: What did you learn in this process of feedback and revision?

A: I learned that I need to get better at writing action scenes, but that I'm good at writing descriptions.

Q: What advice would you give writers who may not enjoy revising?

A: For writers who don't enjoy revision, I'd say that I don't like it, either, but that it's better to get it over with than postpone it.

Q: What are your writing goals?

A: My writing goals are to make other people happy by reading my stories because I love reading other people's, and also to express the stories I have inside me.

Three Gnomes and a Crow

by

Ember Summer

*N*ow dears, quiet down and I'll tell you a story. Of course it's real! What would make you think it's not? Your mother? Tell her that she enjoyed them when she was a child, so she should let you enjoy them, too. Anyway, as I was saying, this is a perfectly real story about a perfectly real adventure which three gnomish–what? Gnomes are real, darling. Anyone who tells you different is selling something. Anyway, back to the story–three gnomish children undertake, and the–stop fidgeting! If you listen to my story all the way through, I'll give you a cookie, all right? Now, where was I? Oh, yes. The story. Well, it's called "Three Gnomes and a Crow"–yes, it is real. Even real stories can have names–anyway, I'll just–no, it isn't that long. You can go play soon– ahem. Here goes. Noma, Litie, and Sovan shared a room . . .

Noma, Litie, and Sovan shared a room in their family's underground house. The room was circular, with a few roots poking into smooth earthen walls, and a bright knotted rug covering the dirt floor. Three

little hawthorn-wood beds, about seven inches long, stood in a curved row against the left wall. Three wardrobes stood against the right wall, and the back of the room was piled with small objects: a pine needle, a shard of glass, a dried hawthorn berry. There was a candle, now out, sitting near Litie's bed, which filled the room with merry light when lit. A small door was set in the wall, leading into a hallway with alcoves every few inches that held small candles to light the way. Along the hall to the left was the bedroom of their parents, Candytuft and Spruce. To the right, the hallway led downwards to the sitting room and a doorway from that led to the kitchen. A short hallway led up to a mudroom, with a door to the Outside.

Capital letter O, in Outside. What is a capital letter? Ask your teacher, darling. Please, let me talk. Noma began stirring . . .

NOMA BEGAN STIRRING, and yawned, blinking her eyes slowly. She sat up, her hazel brown hair in a long braid that reached the center of her back. She blinked her green eyes again and put her feet tentatively on the floor. The dirt was smooth and cold and she shivered in her white nightdress. She stood up and quickly walked to her wardrobe, where she dressed in soft spider-silk tights and undershirt, over which she wore a pair of black wool pants, wool socks, two cotton petticoats, a white cotton underdress that reached to her knees, a red wool overdress that reached her ankles, and, after unbraiding, brushing, and re-braiding her hair, a pointed red wool cap.

She peeked outside into the hall and looked at the grandfather clock across from her. It read six thirty. She let out a soft "Oh!" and hurried back into her room to wake Litie and Sovan.

*W*hat? Less description and more action? Who is telling this story? I like description, don't you? But, yes, there will be action eventually, so just be patient. After dressing . . .

AFTER DRESSING, they all walked down the hall to the kitchen, from where the tantalizing smell of acorncakes was drifting. The kitchen was warm, as Candytuft had built a fire and was busy with breakfast preparations. As Noma, Litie, and Sovan tumbled into the kitchen, Candytuft turned around, smiling at them.

"The acorncakes will be ready soon. Do you want honey, salmonberry jelly, or maple syrup?"

"Honey!" said Sovan.

"Jelly!" said Litie.

"Can I have snowberry jam?" asked Noma.

"I'm sorry dear, but we're all out. If you go pick some snowberries today, I can make more."

"Yes, I'll go after breakfast! Can I have syrup then?"

"'Mkay. Here you are!" She lifted three acorncakes onto three wooden plates and passed them to each gnomish child. "And here's milk." She handed them each a wooden cup filled with frothy milk. "Eat quickly. Then you can go Outside. Just remember–"

"Watch out for the crows and if we need help, call for 'Emer the Wandering Trader.' I know, I know," said Noma.

"Yes, dear." Candy smiled proudly, then went on. "Good news!"

"What?" asked Litie and Noma excitedly. Sovan was too busy smearing honey on his face to answer.

"It snowed! And Sovan, try not to get food all over." She grabbed a scrap of blue cloth, dipped it in water, and cleaned off his

face.

Litie and Noma finished their cakes quickly and washed their plates, then Candy kissed them goodbye and told Noma to be in charge, as she was the eldest. The three siblings put on their boots, hats, scarves, mittens, and coats, and at last were Outside.

Snow had frosted the maples and made them look as fragile as Christmas ornaments. Several of the firs and cedars looked like wedding cakes with droopy green sides, with snow on just a few outside limbs. The dull brown trunks of the trees stood out against the blinding white of the snow, and the bushes' branches held little rivulets of snow that fell off with each slight breath of wind. There were no clouds in the piercing blue, and it was frigid cold. As Noma took a breath, her nose tingled and stung with cold freshness. Why, the whole world looked as if it had been made anew, wiped of all color, a blank canvas Mother Earth would use to rewrite the world's story.

Noma felt bad about marring the beautiful landscape, but her younger siblings had no such inhibitions. As soon as they stepped out the door, Sovan made a snowball and threw it at Litie, eliciting a scream. Noma watched the following battle ensue with a kind of detached distance, not wanting to be dragged in and get snow on her new coat. But she was spared the decision by a mis-thrown snowball, which hit her right in the nose.

"Sovan!" she screamed, and launched herself into the battle.

A short time later, three tired and snowy gnome children began to march through the glorious forest wonderland. This was plenty difficult, as the snow was about as deep as Noma, but it didn't stop her from looking up at the sky every once in a while, looking for crows. Crows were the gnomes' main predators and quite dangerous, and

Thimble Wood was on the outskirts of one crow's territory. The crow didn't venture there often, but there was still the threat, so between searching for predators and stumbling through the snow, she didn't have much time to think. Then Litie remembered something.

"Aren't we supposed to be collecting snowberries?"

"Mm," said Sovan contentedly, his rosy cheeks stretching into a smile at the thought of acorncakes and snowberry jelly, but Noma stopped, her eyes widening.

"Well then, where are the baskets?" began Litie.

Noma slapped one mittened hand to her forehead and began thinking aloud. "I could run back while you and Sovan stay here . . . No, it's too dangerous. How long have we been walking? I'd say near an hour. Sovan, don't you have a friend near here with a mouse carriage?"

"'Mhm. Her name's Issy, and she has a really cool house that I kind of want and a lot of cool toys and some other really cool stuff," said Sovan. Then his face tightened, thinking. "But they don't have snowberry jam or acorncakes," he said finally.

"Great! We can go there and—what is it, Litie?" said Noma exasperatedly, for Litie had scrunched up her face as if she were trying not to laugh, and she was tugging on Noma's arm.

When Noma turned around, she saw a familiar face.

"Candy? What are you . . . ?"

"You forgot the baskets, and your lunch, so I decided to bring it to you. Here!" Candytuft held out three gathering baskets and a picnic basket, gave each of them a hug, and hurried off, calling over her shoulder, "See you at home!"

Noma stood there, holding the four baskets, as Litie laughed

and laughed and Sovan tried to sneak a raspberry tart out of the picnic basket. Noma came to her senses just in time to see him open his mouth . . . and bite down on thin air.

"Don't you eat this till lunch!" she scolded, placing it back in its rightful home. "Now, each of you take one of these gathering baskets and let's go to Thimble Wood!" And they began their tramping once more.

Noma scanned the skies automatically, almost missing the dark shadow on the horizon. She looked up, looked down, bored, then her head flew up again. She thought . . . yes, there it was, a crow.

"Hide," she said quickly, grabbing Litie and Sovan's shoulders and pushing them into the overhanging sword fern, knocking snow on their heads.

She was sure the crow hadn't spotted them, but she made sure they stayed under the fern until she was sure it was completely gone, and even then went on a different, longer path with more protection from the sky. Danger was as sure as the sun would rise each and every day for the gnomes, so she did want to be careful.

Cookies already? Well, okay. The story's only about halfway done. Yes, David, only half. Hurry along, for I won't be stopping any more times. Where are the cookies? Top shelf, next to the cinnamon. All ready? Well, I'll continue then . . .

WHEN THEY FINALLY REACHED THE PATCH, Noma grabbed a snowberry a sixth of her size and proceeded to pick it (or try to): hanging on it, yanking it, and otherwise trying to pull it off its stem. When she finally pulled it off, it fell in the snow, sending up a wave and dousing her with particles of frozen water, and she wished, not for the first or last time, that she were the size of the Big People—then she wouldn't need to go through so much work to get just one snowberry. She reached for the next, but paused, scanning the sky. There were a few clouds and a sparrow—nothing interesting. She sighed, and in doing so almost missed the agonizing scream Sovan let out as the beak of a giant crow closed around him.

It's fine, darlings. He's going to be okay. Don't worry. Oh, you're not worrying? Then why the scrunched face? Hush, he'll be all right. Noma spun around . . .

NOMA SPUN AROUND, dropping her basket and spilling the snowberries inside. About five feet away from her was a pitch-black crow. Its eyes were like sparkling beads of ebony and each feather was a little abyss. In its beak was Sovan, his green cap askew, kicking and screaming and pounding its beak with his fists. The crow looked around, gave a muffled *Caw!* and opened its wings wide.

"Sovan!" screamed Noma, thinking, *Of course this happened, this is all my fault, why did we come here? Snowberries aren't as important as Sovan! How am I going to explain this to Candy? Wait, I should be thinking of a plan!*

She looked around wildly, and saw Litie holding on to the crow's talon. *Even Litie's more courageous than I,* thought Noma desperately as she watched the crow's futile attempts to throw Litie away.

Then Noma was off and running at the crow, and with the downbeat of its wing she grabbed hold of the main flight feathers

and was tossed in the air. The crow screamed in frustration and fumbled Sovan, but caught him just as he fell. It flipped the wing holding Noma upward, and the slippery gloss of the feathers made it impossible to hold on; Noma let go. The air rushed past her, making her eyes water and knocking off her red hat, before she landed on the shining lustery back of the crow.

She slid down but managed to grab hold of some feathers, and hung there as she caught her breath.

"Litie, tie the crow's legs together so it can't take off!"

The crow seemed just able to fly, even with all three of them weighing it down. As Litie disappeared out of Noma's field of vision, Noma started to pull herself towards the crow's neck as it thrashed around. She finally reached its neck and tried to choke it into dropping Sovan. She squeezed and squeezed and finally, with a cry, the crow submitted and dropped Sovan. Noma relaxed and fell off into the cold snow, which eased her sweaty back. She watched the crow take off into the bright blue sky, clearly looking for easier prey, then looked over at Sovan. He had a cut on his right arm and looked shaken, but was sitting up drinking something from Litie; Noma couldn't see what. She groaned and stood up, then walked over to Litie. Litie looked up, and when she saw Noma she frowned. "Why did you send me to get rope if you were just going to let the crow go?"

"Sorry," said Noma sheepishly. "I didn't have the strength to keep it down, and even if we had, what would we do with it?"

"The guy I got the rope from said he could use a crow . . . at least, that's what I think he said. I called for Emer, like Candy said to do, and he has a goat and lots of cool things. He gave this drink to give to Sovan." Litie held up a glass vial filled with reddish liquid.

"Emer also said he can take up home so Candy can look after Sovan."

"Wonderful. Where is he?"

"Right'n behind'a, Miss." Noma turned, startled, and let out a little shriek, for she was looking straight into the eye of a goat.

Now, Noma was only six inches tall, so the goat was much, much bigger than her. It had cocked its head and bent down to sniff her. Its eye, light green and about the size of her head, looked at her curiously. It had a line of darker brown fur down the side of its face, and little horn nubs sticking out of the top of its head.

"Hallo, young'n Miss. I see you're admiring'n m' goat."

Noma startled again and turned towards him. "Oh, uh . . . yes," she said. She only reached his knee, and had to strain to look up at him.

"Her name's Rose'n my name's Emer. Yer sistuh tol' me that your'n name's Noma, righ'?" He had a very jolly round face that looked as if it'd never seen a frown, and curly golden hair, and a very funny way of talking, but Noma stifled her laughter; she knew it wasn't polite to laugh at others.

A lesson you all could learn from. No, this isn't a moral story, but you can still learn lessons from it, David. And you too, Laura. Now, don't interrupt any more—what? I never interrupt any stories, especially not to tell children good moral life lessons. Don't interrupt. Noma said, "Okay, our house is near . . . "

"Yes. Litie told me you can take us to our house. Thank you."

"Ah, 'ts nuh'in'. Where's your'n house?"

"Near the old oak tree, the one that the unicorn used to live by."

"Kay'nee then, I'll'n take y' there'n. Hop up, I'll'ee help."

Noma ran to get the baskets of snowberries and soon they were all sitting on the back of Rose, in a line from Noma down to Sovan. For the first time, Noma was taller than the ferns! The snow looked as soft and puffy as clouds, now that she didn't have to slog through it. The goat was much faster than their little legs, and in no time they were dismounting at their front door. With many farewells and promises to see each other again they parted ways, and Noma, Litie, and Sovan were greeted with a blast of warm air and hugs from Candytuft. The first thing she said to them, once they'd taken off their things and were standing in the kitchen, was, "Where is my picnic basket?"

Noma stood stock still, her eyes widening as she remembered what she'd forgotten.

"In the snowberry patch. But, I have a good reason for it. Sovan was almost eaten!" To cries of horror and "tell me more"s, Noma sat down and began to tell this story.

*T*he end. You want more? Come tomorrow night and I'll tell you the story of the "Three Hares and a Duck," another very true story. Goodbye, darlings! I'll see you tomorrow night.

Three siblings walked in
A forest green. Beware crows
Who can attack. Deadly.

Endings

Polly Alice McCann aided Nuala Kilroy in a revision using existing patterns in Nuala's poem, "Blue Doesn't Have a Smell," to set up an intriguing ending.

Dear Reader,

Nuala's "Blue Doesn't Have a Smell" is a fun title and a fun poem. I see it as a poem about poetry. What is more fun than that? I enjoyed thinking about the stanzas in Nuala's poem and how intentional they are in the jobs that they do for the poem.

When I write poems, I stop to look at where I see patterns. Often, I find something I do that is not on purpose, but I really enjoy very much. (Poems are smarter than poets this way.) So, I look for what the poem is doing and then I try to follow its lead.

Endings are important in any poem. Yes, there is the ending of each line (I like to check and make sure I like the last word on each line). The last word sort of sits out there and gets noticed. There is also the ending of the whole poem—the last stanza, or even the last line.

Nuala's poem has four distinct sections that make the poem build in complexity as it goes along. Together, we focused on how this increase in complexity could make a satisfying ending. We considered the question: "Does the ending do for the poem what the beginning promises it might do?"

The final section is about metaphor. This is where the voice in the poem gives a true analogy comparing flowery language to a whole garden in the mind. This is the end! Each stanza has been building to this moment. To me, this is where the poem opens up. What a wonderful ending. We see the world of words as a garden ready to explore, eat from, live off of, and use creatively. I discovered that this could be called an adjective metaphor or a synesthetic metaphor where senses are crossed like color instead of smell.

To me, this poem is like a doorway to more poetry. The voice in the poem insists she is ready to walk a road less traveled for the pursuit of playing with language. If you like the style or form of Nuala's poem, you can try to recreate another doorway poem with an ending metaphor. Can you do it intentionally? Or try taking the last line of a poem and writing a whole new poem. This is a fun game that poets try all the time to generate unexpected results.

I hope this helps you on your poetry journey!

Polly Alice McCann

Polly Alice McCann grew up in the heartland of the U.S. When she wasn't up in a cottonwood tree reading a book, or trailblazing with her mom's sewing scissors, she spent most of her time "making something." She began art classes at the Nelson-Atkins Museum in Kansas City before her Buster Browns ever reached the floor. Polly graduated from Messiah College with a degree in studio art, then with her MA in Writing for Children and Young Adults at Hamline University in 2011. She is a published poet and author, an adjunct English professor, and loves spending time painting in her studio. Polly thinks writing with kids is all about exploring our imaginations, and creating new places, new worlds, and new friends. Her favorite animals are goats, unicorns, and mermaids. She is always planning the next adventure to share with her family. They have an enormous coonhound dog and live by a bridge over a stream. Check out her children's illustrations at *www.pollymadison.com*.

Nuala Kilroy

Nuala is a young writer who lives in Arlington, Massachusetts. She enjoys writing both poetry and fictional short stories. Currently homeschooled, she fills her days with horse riding, dancing, cuddling her dog, and endless piles of books—more often than not accompanied by a steaming mug of tea. She has always liked writing and words (especially obscure or older words that no one else around her understands). Her favorite authors are J.K. Rowling and Roald Dahl, but she'll read just about anything you put in front of her. That is, as long as her four siblings aren't getting in the way.

Polly Alice McCann: What does your name mean or how did you get it?
Nuala Kilroy: My name is Nuala (pronounced "Nula"). I think it actually means "shoulder," derivative of the name Fianuala, which means "fair shoulder."

Q: Tell us a bit about your family or pets.
A: I have four siblings: an older brother, an older sister, and two younger brothers. So my house is pretty hectic all the time. I got a dog a little under a year ago named Fred.

Q: Who is your fave author or poet?
A: My favorite poets are Shel Silverstein and also I really like Edgar Allan Poe.

Q: What do you do for fun?

A: I like to write, obviously. I also like reading, dancing, horseback riding, and photography.

Q: Fave food or place to eat?

A: I think my favorite food is probably watermelon. I like any sweet fruit, or chocolate.

Q: What is the craziest thing about the city you live in?

A: There is a lot of historical stuff from the Revolutionary War, and historical monuments. Around town, there are these little stones—engraved on them are snippets of writing about people from the Revolutionary War and what happened to them.

Q: What is your favorite word?

A: I don't know if I can choose just one. But I like using obscure words and old slang from the '20s to the '50s. Rich people who lived luxurious lifestyles used to be called "eggs."

Blue Doesn't Have a Smell

by
Nuala Kilroy

S ometimes
I use words
that don't make too much sense
because really
darkness isn't a place
and red lipstick can't describe a feeling
and blue doesn't have a smell

But sometimes
this world is too tough
And sometimes
I need it to be a little softer

so I call sunlight
golden honey
because then it seems sweet
instead of scalding

so I call snowfall
fairy dust
because then it seems magical
instead of cold

Sometimes
this world is too bland
And sometimes
I need it to be a little more exciting

so I say pillows
feel like clouds
because then I'm flying
instead of just falling asleep

so I say good food
is like ambrosia
because then I'm a goddess
instead of just human

so when people say that my words
are pretentious
or nonsensical
or showy
I like to say

that I prefer flowery
because then it seems like

they might be growing
in a garden
in my brain.